Advanced Praise for *Candy Ca...*

"Sublimely drawn characters fuel a slasher romp that delivers the goods. While the author satisfies the genre by showcasing the brutal murders, there's ample suspense, as a genuinely scary killer roams the property during a snowstorm that makes escape an unlikely option."

— *Kirkus Reviews*

"With great characters, including authentic LGBTQ and disability representation, multiple points of view, original, bloody, and cinematic kills, a fresh and twisty story with just the right amount of nostalgia, and a perfect dose of dark humor, this book is exactly what it claims to be, "Goosebumps for Grown-ups," and oh, what fun that is for horror readers."

— *Booklist*

"Great deaths, a creepy villain and believably written characters–this is a masterclass in slasher fiction."

— *FanFiAddict*

"Hark! Hear Brian McAuley sing! Glory to his newborn slasher's swing! Peace on earth and mercy have gone away, 'cause Candy Cain is here to slay!"

— Clay McLeod Chapman, author of
What Kind of Mother and *Ghost Eaters*

"While I'm not saying that enjoying this blood-soaked book will land you on Santa's naughty list, I am saying that reading *Candy Cain Kills* is absolutely worth the lump of coal you'll find in your stocking. McAuley's ability to craft a page-turner is unrivalled. I have no doubt that reading this book will quickly become every horror fan's favourite Christmas tradition."

— Caitlin Marceau, award-winning
author of *This Is Where We Talk Things Out*

"This Christmas slasher, in the vein of movies like *Silent Night, Deadly Night*, is a quick read and a perfect book for gorehounds to devour on a cold Christmas night where there's a fire in the hearth, some cocoa on the nightstand, and possibly something murderous in the snowy dark."

— *Library Journal*

"Brian McAuley has quickly earned a spot on my Must-Read list. His fiction has a cinematic quality, and you're guaranteed a good time!"

— Brian Keene

"Brian McAuley is a horror mastermind, a rowdy and ruthless writer capable of killing anything on the page. In his slasher sendoff, Candy Cain Kills, you can tell he's having the time of his life in all that blood-drenched snow. When McAuley writes, he's channeling the canon as much as he is carving a slice of his own. This book is a single-sitting, sweat-drenched thrill."

— Michael J. Seidlinger, author of *The Body Harvest* and *Anybody Home?*

Praise for *Curse of the Reaper*

"McAuley excels at balancing the psychological against the supernatural, but he's even better at satirizing the Hollywood machine. *Curse of the Reaper* is a very funny book... but when McAuley turns to horror in earnest, he goes hard."

— *Esquire*'s Best Horror Books of 2022

"At times deliriously fun and delightfully gory. Its blood-filled heart, however, is its main characters and their personal struggles... This book is a must for fans of the slasher genre."

"*Curse of the Reaper* is sinister in execution, creeping through each chapter until the sharp blade of carefully revealed plot twists cuts deep into our psyche... it pulls the reader in and doesn't let go until it consumes them."

CANDY CAIN KILLS

BRIAN McAULEY

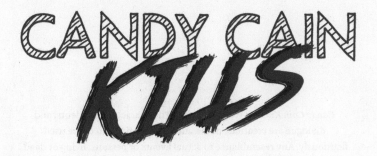

KILLER VHS SERIES
BOOK 2

SHORTWAVE
PUBLISHING

Copyright © 2023 by Brian McAuley

Cover design by Marc Vuletich and Alan Lastufka.
Interior design by Alan Lastufka.

First Edition published November 2023.

10 9 8 7 6 5 4 3 2 1

ISBN 978-1-959565-19-2 (Paperback)
ISBN 978-1-959565-20-8 (eBook)

For the naughty ones.

CHAPTER ONE

*L**ooks a lot less haunted now.*

That's Rick's first thought as he drives up to the gray stone cottage in the middle of the dense woods. He's proud of the restoration he pulled off, despite the quick timeline and tight funding.

Of course, most of the work he did was on the inside, but Lynette was right about putting that white trellis next to the new front porch. It added some welcome charm, even if the pink bougainvillea he snaked through the wood was going to be dead within a week from the bitter cold. She said it was all about first impressions, and Rick understands that now as he pulls his truck around to the back of the house.

He's been a handyman for years, but he's never spearheaded his own renovation project, handling every little detail himself. If Lynette had paid him enough, he probably would've hired a team, done things a bit more up-to-code. The most he could afford to outsource on this job was getting his pal Ned to help with the plumbing in exchange for a case of beer. Other than that, it was Rick who took that heap of a Thornton place and turned it into a rentable property from the abandoned shell it once was.

Not just abandoned. Haunted.

Rick puts the brakes on the H-word again, throwing the shifter into *Park* beside the basement bulkhead. No way he had the scratch to replace those rusty storm doors, but Lynette said the back of the house wasn't a priority. Fixing up the cellar on the other side of those doors was more important, and that's where Rick's work would finally come to an end.

He needs the strength of both arms just to pull one of those heavy suckers open on its creaky hinges. When he does, a stench comes rolling out to greet him, and he nearly coughs up his morning coffee. More than likely a critter snuck in and died down there in the earthy tomb of the root cellar.

Rick drags his toolbox from the truck bed, clicks his flashlight on, and takes the stony steps one at a time. The ceiling must be just under six feet high because at six one, he has to keep his shoulders hunched and his head down as he navigates the space.

He shines his light through the blackness of the cellar, which runs the entirety of the floor space above with a handful of stone support beams keeping the place from falling in on itself. It still feels like that could happen at a moment's notice, and Rick really wishes he didn't have to spend three days working in this death trap.

But Lynette has been very clear. Because the cottage is so "cozy" (real estate talk for "cramped"), she wants this basement to be finished and converted into a storage space for any potential long-term renters. Rick figures at the very least he can lay down some loose boards over the dirt and make it feel a little less like a grave. He doesn't have time for much else, but he can see some storage shelves already lining the far wall, packed with boxes and cans and Mason jars. Maybe it's the grub gone bad giving off that rotten smell. If he clears the shelves and tosses the food, that's two birds with one stone: making some space and killing the stink.

He lowers his metal toolbox to the floor and starts toward the rickety wooden staircase that leads back up into the house. A quick inspection of the steps shows the wood is rotting to hell, but there's no sign of termites. He should be able to get away with not replacing the whole damn thing, which is great, because he definitely doesn't have time for that. Then again, if some renter's rug rat comes running down the steps and breaks their leg through a busted board, Lynette will have Rick's ass. He tests his full weight on each step until he arrives safely at the top, deciding it's probably safe to leave them be.

The basement door opens out into the living room, which feels bright and airy now with white walls and exposed beams in the ceiling above. This had definitely been the hardest space to renovate.

This is where the fire happened.

Rick was expecting more structural damage when he first started the job, but these old stone houses were built tough. He did have to pry up all those blackened floorboards, and it was hard not to notice the spots where the bodies had left behind a sticky tar-like residue. But after he replaced those hardwoods and fixed up the scorched walls and ceiling, you'd never know what happened here ten years ago.

Rick grew up thirty miles east of Nodland, but he remembers hearing the legend as a teenager.

The story of a family who died on Christmas morning, leaving this burned-out heap in their wake. But if the tales were true, it wasn't the tree fire that killed them. They were stone-cold murdered by...

Rick shivers, not letting the name light up his brain for fear of summoning a ghost.

He'd spent the last few months keeping the gruesome legend at bay, knowing that if he thought for one full minute about what happened here, he'd be too damned spooked to get the job done. He's too close to the end to cave now.

In the kitchen, every cabinet had been stripped and stained, all the old appliances refurbished back into working shape.

"Shabby chic," Lynette kept saying. Rick didn't know what that meant until he watched her swoop in to decorate each room in his wake. As far as he could tell, "shabby chic" was code for "make cheap look antique so we can charge more."

He grabs a can of beer from the six pack he placed in the "vintage" fridge yesterday, cracks the tab and takes a swig.

Once he's done here today, he'll head over to the diner for a hot meal and more cold beers. Grace will be working tonight, like most nights.

"The usual, Rick?" she'll ask. He loves that, being a

regular; but he thinks, he hopes, maybe it's more than that. Maybe there's something real there.

It started with small talk, like with any other waitress, but there were some nights when Grace would prop her elbows up on that counter and share every thought in her head with Rick. He'd listen and share right back, things he'd never talked about with anybody. Turns out they both had dreams of moving to Los Angeles, but both were just too scared to make a go of it alone. They'd get lost in conversation, building their hypothetical lives side by side, until Grace's boss would remind her there were other customers in need of service.

Maybe Rick is fooling himself, and she's just killing idle time; but he really feels like maybe, just maybe, he and Grace have a shot at building a life together. He's made up his mind that tonight is the night he's finally going to ask her out on a proper—

Clang.

The sound echoes up from the open basement door.

Better not be those brand-new pipes or Ned's gonna owe him more than a case of beer.

Rick brings his half-empty can down the steps, back into the dank cellar. He clicks his flashlight on and moves it over the dark. Scanning those support beams sends tall shadows across the dirt.

One shadow separates from another and darts toward him.

He stumbles back, but the raccoon just squeals as it runs up the stone steps, back out of the storm door Rick had left open. He finally catches his breath and laughs. When he pulls the metal door closed, he's extra careful not to let the weight of it come crashing down on his head.

Man, he's extra spooked today. Motivation to work twice as fast so he can get the hell out of here and on that stool in front of sweet Grace and her pretty face.

Hey, that rhymes. Maybe he'll write a song about her someday. Get guitar lessons in Los Angeles.

Rick looks down at his toolbox and notices the metal lid is swung open.

That was the sound he heard; he's sure of it now.

Could a raccoon have done that? They're notorious with trash can lids, but it's hard to imagine those little mitts navigating the latch on his toolbox.

He takes a knee to inspect the contents and senses right away that something is wrong. He knows every single tool in this box because they'd all been handed down by his father, who handed them down from *his* father.

"If you take good care of your tools, you'll never need to replace them," father told son, who told son.

That's how Rick knows that his claw hammer is gone; and he sure as hell didn't see the tool clutched in that raccoon's paw as it ran up the steps.

No, that hammer is currently in the grip of a hand, extending from a tall shape that's bleeding out of the darkness behind Rick now. Before he has a chance to turn and face the tool thief, a piercing cold explodes at the back of his skull.

The dark room flashes blinding white, and Rick collapses forward on top of his toolbox.

He reaches back to touch the crown of his head,

which feels like a hardboiled egg that's been cracked against a countertop. Bits of wet eggshell peel away against his fingertips. When he moves his hand back in front of his eyes to see the bloody white flakes, his battered brain suddenly kicks in:

Not eggshell, numbnuts. Skull bone.

A gushing warmth flows down the back of his neck, cold awareness washing over him.

I'm bleeding. Someone hit me.

He reaches below his belly for a weapon from the toolbox, pulling a wrench and swiping it backwards through the air. A human-sized shadow dodges the clumsy swing, ducking behind one of those stone pillars with an awful sound.

Laughter.

Raccoons don't laugh.

Rick pushes up to his feet, turns and falls back to his knees. He stumbles once more, but a wire must've popped loose in that exposed brain of his because his body won't do what he tells it to. The best he can manage is an army crawl toward those rickety stairs.

More *clangs* of metal on metal, followed by a raspy voice.

"Presents."

The hammer-wielder must be rummaging through the toolbox again, but Rick's already clawed himself halfway up the wooden steps. Splinters slide under his fingernails, but he can't let that stop him.

His left calf feels it first, the cold metal piercing through flesh. Either the Phillips-head or the flathead, he figures. It doesn't really matter which one, because the other screwdriver sinks straight through his right leg next, completing the pair. The sheer force of that second blow snaps the rotten wood plank beneath, which means he probably should have replaced the staircase after all.

Rick really is proud of all the work he did to bring this house back to life. He likes to think his dad would be proud too, and his dad's dad before him. He'll take that pride to his grave, and maybe see them both beyond. He'll also take with him the silent knowledge that the Thornton place really is haunted after all.

The legend is true.

Pain pulses from his leg up to his head and back down his other leg in an endless electrical circuit; but the worst sensation of all is the presence hovering over him. Breathing behind his ear to whisper in the dark.

"Nice boy."

A hand strokes Rick's blood-soaked hair.

He can't help thinking about that poor family coming to spend Christmas here. He wishes he could warn them, but the black paint of eternal dark is already dripping over his vision.

The claw end of the hammer arcs down and finds a home in Rick's fractured skull, punctuating the final thought in his punctured brain.

Candy Cain is real.

CHAPTER TWO

"Austin, help your sister."

His parents' favorite refrain. Austin's heard it a million times a day, ever since Fiona was born twelve years ago. This time, Mom is saying it over her shoulder from the passenger seat of the family station wagon. Dad's busy double-checking the printed MapQuest directions from behind the wheel while they're parked at a gas station in the middle of nowhere.

Austin glances across the back seat to see Fiona already opening the car door, trying to get her cane out onto the pavement so she can lean her weight on it.

"I don't need help," she says. *Her* favorite refrain.

Austin sighs, climbing out and moving around the back of the station wagon. The boxy trunk is packed to the brim, but it's *his* bag that's being crushed under all the others. Typical.

Fiona nearly tumbles across the pavement just as Austin rushes up; but she catches herself, stabilizing with the cane in one hand while waving her brother away with the other.

"I'm good," she says, gripping the black cane handle. "Just messing with you."

"Yeah, right." Austin watches his sister slowly cane her way under the rusty overhang toward the restroom door.

After a jiggle of the handle, Fiona reads the little sign aloud. "Ask attendant for key."

She's about to start the long journey toward the convenience store when Austin puts up an open palm. "Just chill. I'll get it."

Inside he finds a grizzled man in a camouflage cap watching a small television set behind the counter.

"Excuse me?" Austin asks over the sounds of desert warfare blaring from the small speakers. "May I have the key to the restroom?"

The man doesn't look Austin in the eye, keeps his gaze glued to the televised carnage as he reaches beneath the counter. For a shotgun? No, just a wooden block with a key dangling off the end.

"Read it," the gas man grunts, tossing the key-block over the counter.

Austin catches it, looks at the message scrawled in Sharpie across the wood.

DON'T LOCK KEY IN SHITHOUSE, SHITHEAD.

He stifles a laugh, walking back outside to his sister.

"I could've gotten it," she says.

"Well, I'd like to get where we're going sometime before Christmas."

Fiona rolls her eyes as she grabs the key and disappears into the bathroom.

Austin leans his back against the gas station wall and

looks up at the big pine trees towering overhead. He isn't used to seeing this terrain so close to home. Dad said the drive would only take a couple of hours, but constant rest stops for pee breaks and map checks have slowed them down. They're only a few miles into the San Bernardino mountains, but it's already a solid ten degrees colder than Los Angeles, and Austin misses that warmth.

Staring at the rugged landscape, it's hard not to think about that movie, and the absolutely awful timing of this little family trip.

Just two nights ago, Austin and his friends went out for their regular Friday night movie ritual. Usually, this meant yelling at the screen during some trashy horror remake that Ethan picked. But sometimes Mateo, an aspiring arthouse filmmaker, would insist on something a bit more cultured. Austin didn't know much about the film his best friend was dragging them to see at the Aero Theater that night, other than maybe it was a Western?

Brokeback Mountain was not a Western.

It was a big-screen mirror, reflecting all the thoughts and feelings that had been silently stirring in Austin for years. Seeing those two men together on the screen made him excited and scared and sad in swirling waves until the lights finally came on, finding Austin frozen in the theater seat, exposed like a raw nerve.

Valerie stood first with a big yawn. "Well, that was boring as shit. Let's go back to my house and get crunk."

Part two of the Friday ritual involved going back to Valerie's basement for suburban debauchery. Predictably, Valerie drank too much that night and threw up, so Mateo had to put his girlfriend to bed early. Equally predictable was Ethan getting so stoned on skunk weed that he passed out on the basement couch.

When Mateo came back downstairs, he suggested they chill outside; and that's how Austin found himself sitting in the grass with his best friend, a bottle of Captain Morgan between them, and a whole lot of butterflies swarming in his gut.

Growing up down the street from each other, Austin and Mateo were inseparable from an early age. They'd ride their bikes to school, play video games after, watch obscure foreign films on DVD during endless sleepovers. Austin couldn't imagine his life without Mateo; but it was junior year, and college applications were bringing that reality into focus. Mateo was destined for NYU film school, while Austin's family couldn't afford anything outside of Cal State. The more Austin thought about losing Mateo, the more he realized how deep his feelings ran.

"What'd you think of the movie?" Mateo finally asked, passing the bottle.

"It was good, yeah." Austin gulped the spicy amber liquid.

"Pretty hot, huh?"

Austin couldn't tell if Mateo was joking, so he played it safe as he passed the bottle back. "Yeah. I can't believe Anne Hathaway showed her boobs. So cool."

Mateo laughed and took a bigger swig of rum. "I'm not talking about Anne Hathaway."

He held the bottle out, looking Austin directly in the eye. Austin's mouth went dry as he reached for it, placing his hand on Mateo's. They stayed like that, hands clasped together around the glass for what felt like an eternity until Austin couldn't take it anymore.

He lurched forward and placed a sloppy kiss on Mateo's lips.

Before either of them could speak, the sliding glass door zipped open behind them.

"Mateo," the puke-mouthed zombie groaned.

Mateo leapt to his feet. "Valerie."

"Come snuggle me."

While Mateo hurried to help his drunk girlfriend back up to bed, Austin just sat and stared at the flamboyant pirate on the rum label, feeling like a total idiot. No way was he sticking around until morning for the awkwardness that would ensue. He took the Captain with him and walked the three miles home.

When he woke up with a raging hangover and remembered what he'd done, he wanted to crawl out of his skin. But he knew he couldn't run from this; he couldn't hide his feelings anymore. He figured he and Mateo could talk it out that day, for better or worse; but when Austin went downstairs, he found his whole family gathered in the living room.

"Another family meeting," Fiona explained, eating a bowl of Corn Pops on the couch.

"Your father has a surprise for us." Mom leaned against the wall and sipped her coffee.

Dad swiveled around in the computer chair to face them. "I booked us a house on the internet."

"I don't think we're all gonna fit in there." Fiona

pointed her spoon at the Dell desktop over Dad's shoulder.

"Very funny," Dad said. "Come on, take a look. It's out near Big Bear." He scrolled through the internet posting. "A remote little getaway in the mountains. We'll get out of LA, have a real winter wonderland Christmas."

Austin stared at the pixelated image of a stone cottage in the middle of the woods. "When are we leaving?" was all he could muster back.

"Tomorrow," Dad responded. "So, we're going to spend today packing together, as a family."

"What if I had plans with my friends for winter break?" Austin asked.

"Your friends aren't going anywhere," Mom said.

"This is going to be good for us," Dad promised. "Some quality time together with no distractions." It sounded like he was trying to convince himself.

Divorce was all the rage, and Austin's parents had been teetering on the brink for far too long. Valerie's parents split last year, and part of Austin wished that his would just get it over with already. They were constantly fighting about money, especially after racking up all those medical bills for Fiona's tests and treatments.

Austin's earliest memories of his sister were of the little baby screaming and crying in pain, his parents obsessively fussing over her day and night. He sympathized with his sister, he really did. He just couldn't help feeling resentful that she soaked up all Mom and Dad's attention with—

Thump.

The sound pulls Austin back to the gas station, where

he leans his ear toward the graffiti-stained bathroom door. "Fiona?"

"I'm fine."

But he can tell from her voice that she isn't fine. He tries to open the door, but he can't without the key. He just has to wait and listen to his sister struggling within until she finally swings the door open, her black hair a tousled mess.

"You fell on your ass, didn't you?" Austin says.

"What? No." She blows the stray strands from in front of her eyes. "I fell on my face."

Austin looks over her shoulder at the grimy bathroom floor. "Gross."

Fiona canes past him, rubbing her cheek against his shirt as she goes.

"Fiona! Gross!"

"Let's go, slowpoke," she calls over her shoulder. "I'd like to get where we're going sometime before Christmas."

Austin huffs as he follows her back to the car.

Dad now has an old map spread out over the dashboard as he checks it against the MapQuest directions. "Maybe they renumbered the route."

"That's not how routes work, Greg." Mom shakes her head. "Why can't you just go inside and ask for directions?"

"Because I know where we're going," Dad insists.

"Isn't she waiting for us?"

"She can wait a little longer."

"I just don't understand how you didn't get a phone number for the house."

"I told you, the number she gave me was for her office. If you ever listened to me, you would. . ."

Dad's eyes catch in the rearview mirror, realizing that Austin and Fiona are already back there.

"Oh, hey." He puts on a big smile. "Ready to roll? We've only got—"

Bang-bang.

Austin jumps in his seat as the store manager thumps his fist against the window.

"Key!" the man shouts through the glass.

Austin turns to Fiona, who shrugs with an "Oops."

Austin rolls down the window. "I'm really sorry, but—"

"Shithead." The man spits tobacco to the pavement.

"Excuse me?" Mom's voice boils with rage.

"Excuse me, sir?" Dad's version is much softer. "Would you be able to point us in the direction of Nodland? It doesn't seem to be on the map."

"That's because they don't wanna *be* on a map. Take 38 North. Turn left on Exodus."

"Thank you very much, sir." Dad rolls up all the windows and starts the engine.

Mom stares at her husband in disbelief. "He calls your son a shithead and you call him *sir?*"

"You wanted directions, Dana." He throws the shifter into drive. "I got them."

Austin isn't bothered by his dad not sticking up for him. He's more bothered that he sees so much of himself in his cowardly father. He wonders if he'll ever have the courage to speak up and tell Mateo how he really feels, or if his best friend will even want to talk to him again after the other night.

He wishes he could just call Mateo now and get it over with, but he'll have to wait until tomorrow to see if he gets the cell phone he asked for.

In this family, Austin actually getting what he wants would be a true Christmas miracle.

CHAPTER THREE

"Looks like we're here!" Dad announces, waking Fiona from another fatigue nap. Her cheek is pressed against the back window when her eyes flutter open to see that the lush green pines have given way to dead brown trunks, slicing through the empty landscape.

No life to be found, let alone a house.

"Where is here, exactly?" Mom asks from the passenger seat, checking the map again.

Dad tugs the wheel, turning down a narrow passage in the dry forest. He points to the rusty old mailbox as they pass. "Lynette said that would be our sign."

Fiona yawns. "Just turn right at the tetanus trap."

Nobody laughs. She swears her family is getting more humorless by the day.

The station wagon moves slowly along the unpaved driveway as Fiona leans forward, looking out the front windshield. The little stone house in the distance grows larger on their approach, and the trellis of flowers really makes it look like something out of a fairytale. But the flowers are all wilted, and kids always get eaten in fairytales.

A woman with more makeup than face stands on the small wooden porch, waving in a crisp beige pantsuit. Her hand keeps flapping as she bops down the steps toward the car before it even stops. "Welcome, welcome!"

Dad gets out to greet her. "I'm so sorry we're late, Lynette."

"No problem at all," Lynette assures him. "I'm just glad you found the place alright. It's a magical escape, wouldn't you say? Tucked away from the modern world."

Fiona pops the door open and steps out with her cane.

"Oh." Lynette whispers, not softly enough. "I didn't realize you had a handicapped child."

"We prefer 'handi-capable,'" Mom says.

"And I prefer 'Fiona,' but who cares what I think?" Fiona shrugs. The only thing more tiring than her disability are the endless shades of patronizing reactions to it. Especially when you're stuck with something as misunderstood as juvenile idiopathic arthritis.

Lynette gives a plastic smile. "It's just, there are quite a few stairs and we aren't equipped for—"

Fiona pushes past Lynette and up the porch steps, making a big show of it. A hundred knives are stabbing into her knees and ankles, but she grits her teeth and bears the flareup, turning back to Lynette with a bitter grin. "How about a tour, Lynette?"

Even with all that makeup, the blush is visible on the woman's cheeks. "Of course."

Fiona is surprised to find the space inside is more cramped than it looks from the outside. The upstairs landing hovers over half of the living room, which would be pretty roomy without the giant Christmas tree in the corner, lit up with twinkling lights.

"Merry Christmas!" Lynette spreads her arms wide like a *Price is Right* girl.

Dad turns to the family with an expectant smile. "I made a special request for the tree, picked out the star topper myself." He points to the sparkling silver star on top of the tree. "We're going to make tomorrow the best Christmas ever! Opening presents by the roaring fire while the snow falls outside."

"Oh." Lynette makes a stink face. "I'm afraid the fireplace is purely decorative."

"Oh." Dad's shoulders slump toward the empty stone hearth. "I just saw it in the photos and thought. . . well, that's okay!"

He's trying so hard, and Fiona really hopes it works. The last thing she wants is to spend her teenage years shuffling between two parents in two houses. The thought exhausts her achy knees as she looks up to the landing above, where a wooden railing runs the length of an open hallway.

"Don't you just love an open concept?" Lynette asks no one in particular as she guides them upstairs.

Fiona puts her cane in her left hand and uses the banister on the right to balance as she takes it one step at a time. Even with the support, it hurts like hell; but she's learned to compartmentalize the pain, box it up inside. The more she shows it, the more *Are you okays* come her way, and those only make her feel a whole lot less okay.

Mom's throwing a worried expression at her right now, but Fiona just smiles to deflect.

"As advertised," Lynette says, approaching the first door, "we have two bedrooms upstairs."

"Two?" Austin asks.

"Don't worry." She opens the door to reveal bunk beds. "This one has two beds."

"I call top bunk," Fiona elbows her brother, who shakes his head in response. They used to have fun ribbing each other back and forth, but he's been so damn moody lately. If that's what puberty meant, Fiona was not looking forward to it.

"Check this out," Lynette opens a door to reveal the double bathroom connecting both bedrooms. "Double sink, double vanity."

Mom frowns at this. "We're sharing a bathroom with the children?"

Dad clears his throat. "Uh, I don't think the listing mentioned that they were connected?"

"Oh?" Lynette cocks her head. "I thought it would be a perk for most families."

Their family was definitely not most families. Fiona didn't realize that until she started spending time at her best friend Molly's house. Molly's parents were always laughing and touching each other. Asking "How are your parents doing, Fiona?" with a concerned furl of the brow. It was actually refreshing to have people more concerned about her dysfunctional family than they were with her dysfunctional body.

"So, Lynette," Mom says, "how long have you been renting this place?"

Fiona recognizes that tone. It's the tone Mom uses when she already suspects the answer and is going to gleefully rub it in Dad's face.

"You're actually my lucky first tenants," Lynette responds.

Bingo. Fiona watches the expected glare shoot from her mother to her father, who looks away. That'll be fodder for a fight later.

"This house used to belong to my brother, but he. . ." Lynette takes a strange pause as she leads them through the bathroom. "He passed away about ten years ago. The estate was just languishing in legal red tape until I finally inherited the place and fixed it up."

"Fixed it up?" Mom asks, her eyes now searching the space for flaws. She's good at finding those. "Was it in bad shape?"

"Update it, I should have said." Lynette guides them into the master bedroom. "For example, putting fresh glass in the glorious skylight above the master bed!" She points up, and the whole family leans over the mattress to look up at. . . grey skies. "On a clear night, you can see all the stars!" Lynette promises.

On that anticlimactic note, they all head back downstairs.

"What is it that you do for a living, Mr. Werner?" Lynette asks.

"Oh, I'm a software engineer."

"Well, I don't know much about computers, but I hear there's lots of money to be made in that industry."

"There can be," Mom interjects, "if you ask for what you're worth."

This is a constant argument between Fiona's parents. Mom insisting that Dad demand a raise or else threaten to quit. Dad insisting he shouldn't rock the boat because he's easily replaceable, and they need the medical benefits for Fiona. Mom reminding him that even with health insurance, they're drowning in out-of-pocket costs from all the therapies and treatments.

Try listening to that fight on repeat and not feeling like a burden.

"Speaking of renovations," Lynette says as they land back in the living room. "The only part of the house that hasn't been fix— uh, updated is the basement." She points to a door. "My contractor was supposed to finish it up this week, but he flaked before the job was done. You just can't trust anyone these days, can you? Anyway, who needs a basement when you've got this spacious kitchen!"

Lynette leads them into the kitchen and opens the old oven, which definitely looks like it's cooked a child or two. "Fully refurbished appliances. I didn't want to mess with the authentic cottage vibes, you know?"

"It's very. . . shabby chic." Mom nearly chokes on the words.

Mom hates shabby chic.

"That's exactly what I was going for!" Lynette lights up. "Were you planning on cooking tonight, Mrs. Werner?"

Mom also hates assumed gender roles.

"Greg?" She turns to Dad. "Were *you* planning on cooking tonight?"

Dad blushes. "I was worried the groceries would go bad on the drive, so I was thinking we'd have dinner in town?" He has a bad habit of posing ideas like questions.

Guess who hates that?

"On Christmas Eve?" Mom asks.

"Well," Lynette says, "there's not much to speak of in Nodland, but I suppose the diner might still be open all night. If not, there's an adorable little general store. Either way, I recommend stocking up on groceries and filling this vintage fridge." Lynette opens the fridge door to reveal a six pack of beer with one can missing. "That contractor, I swear."

"We don't mind cleaning up after him," Austin says, reaching for a can.

Mom swats his hand away. "Very funny."

Lynette gives a very forced laugh, Mom and Dad both joining in. Fiona can't believe her dumb brother is getting more laughs than she is.

"Landline is here on the kitchen wall," Lynette points to the corded phone. "But no cell service, internet, or television. It really is the perfect place to just hunker down and rest for the week." It feels like she's still trying to sell the place. "So why don't I let you get to it? There's just the matter of signing the rental agreement and settling up payment. . ."

"Right, of course." Dad hands Lynette an envelope. She flips through the bills inside while he quickly signs a stack of papers against the wall.

"Wonderful!" Lynette smiles. "Well, I better hit the

road before the snow kicks in. You're in for a white Christmas, so I hope you kids packed your snow gear!"

Fiona serves the false enthusiasm right back to her. "Oh, I just can't wait to make snow angels!"

Lynette doesn't know what to make of the comment, so she just nods and heads out the door.

Austin turns to his sister. "Why do you have to be so uncomfortable?"

"I'm perfectly comfortable," she responds.

Dad claps his hands. "Okay. So, here's what I'm thinking. First, we all wash up."

"One by one in the shared bathroom?" Mom asks.

Dad ignores it. "Then we head into town for dinner, come back here, make hot cocoa and—"

"I call first shower," Austin says, heading for the stairs.

"Not until after you help unpack," Dad calls after him.

Austin sighs, spinning back to come down the stairs while Mom passes him on her way up.

"I'll save some hot water for you," she jokes, ruffling his hair.

Fiona's left alone in the living room when she hears it. A strange hum coming from below the floorboards. She lowers onto her tender knees and puts her ear to the wooden floors.

It's not a mechanical hum. Not electricity or pipes.

It's got notes and rhythm.

Like a person humming a song. Sounds so familiar...

Thunk.

Austin trips over Fiona's cane on the floor and drops the two presents he was carrying.

"What are you doing down there?" he asks.

"I thought I heard something."

"Well, I hope it's Santa bringing more presents. Otherwise, it's gonna be a light Christmas." Austin kicks the two lonely presents beneath the tree. "Those were the only ones in the car."

Fiona is fully aware that her parents' pockets are thin this year. She's also fully aware that the financial strain she creates has an impact on her brother.

"What'd you ask Old Man Claus for this year?" she asks, trying to find some genuine connection with him.

"A cell phone."

Fiona eyes the small box with Austin's name on it. "Size looks promising."

Austin shrugs. "At this point, I'd settle for a one-way sleigh ride out of this hellhole."

He walks away without asking his sister what *she* wants for Christmas.

It's just the one thing, really, but it's probably too much to ask.

Fiona just wants to feel a little less alone in this fractured family.

She puts her ear back to the floor to listen, but the humming is gone.

Not a creature is stirring.

CHAPTER FOUR

D ana offers to drive to dinner, partially to give Greg a break and partially because she doesn't trust him driving in the snow. A solid inch or two is now layering the sleepy town of Nodland as they roll down Main Street. It's a tiny mountain hamlet, not much to speak of outside of an old church that looms high across the street from the red neon sign for the Nodland Diner.

Dana grew up in a small town like this in rural Massachusetts, and she couldn't wait to escape to the big city. Boston first, then Los Angeles to pursue her acting dream. A dream long buried under diapers and bag lunches.

It occurs to her now, climbing out of the station wagon, that if she and Greg don't sort out their finances soon, they might have to leave LA for small-town life again. Greg is trying his best, but a Christmas vacation isn't a solution. It's a diversion. She just wishes she understood his thought process a little better sometimes. The quirky computer programmer she fell in love with could be a bit glitchy.

Dana enters the diner first, all wood-paneled walls and puke-green benches.

"Take a seat anywhere," the waitress says from the behind the counter. "I'll be right with you."

The only other patron in the place is an old man in a black trench coat, hunched over the counter. He taps his fingers on the edge of his coffee cup in a wordless request. Dana knows that one well, having spent years serving tables between auditions. Or maybe it was more accurate to say she did auditions between serving tables. After all, her acting career went nowhere, and she recently picked up the apron again to scrape together some extra cash for the family.

The waitress adds more steaming black coffee to the man's mug as he reaches into his coat, pulls out a flask and taps in some potent whiskey. Now Dana knows *exactly* what kind of customer this guy is, exactly what kind of place her husband brought their family to for dinner on Christmas Eve.

Fiona is about to squeeze into the booth when Austin cuts in front of her. "No way. I'm not getting up and down every time you need to go to the bathroom."

Fiona sighs as Austin gets into the booth first.

Dana misses the days when these two got along. Even when Austin was just a toddler, he would go to his sister when she cried in the middle of the night. Sometimes he'd even sing her back to sleep with a lullaby. Things were so much simpler back then.

"How retro is this place?" Greg slides into the booth across from the kids. He pushes the buttons on the '50s style tabletop jukebox. "Some great tunes in here. Honey, do you have any change?"

"Juke's broken," the waitress says, approaching with plastic menus. "Merry Christmas Eve!"

"Same to you. . ." Greg squints at her name tag. "Grace. Got any specials tonight?"

"We've got a chicken fried steak with sausage gravy. That's a popular one."

"I'll do that, thanks," Greg says.

"Cholesterol," Dana reminds him.

"Christmas," Greg counters, closing his menu.

Dana bites her tongue, flipping through the pages. "I'm not seeing the salad section."

"Oh, we have a mixed green side salad."

Dana foolishly waits to hear more options, but all she gets is a blank smile back, so she closes the menu. "I guess I'm having a mixed green side salad then."

"Ranch, blue cheese, Russian?"

All Dana hears is *fat, fat, fat.* Sticking to her diet is usually hardest during the holidays, but she doesn't feel like she's missing anything special at this particular establishment.

"Oil and vinegar," she responds. "On the side."

"And for the kiddos?"

Dana has to stop herself from ordering for them, an old habit she hasn't quite shaken yet. Austin orders a classic breakfast, bacon crispy, while Fiona asks for blueberry pancakes. They may be getting older, but some things never change.

"You folks just passing through?" Grace asks, collecting the menus.

"No, we're staying in town," Greg answers. "Over on Delilah Road."

"Ah." Grace nods. "The old Thornton house. My friend Rick did the renovations there."

"Well," Dana interjects, "your friend failed to finish the job."

"I'll be sure to let him know." A sudden sadness inches into Grace's voice. "If I ever see him again."

Maybe Lynette wasn't the only one stood up by this contractor. Dana suddenly feels for the young waitress, softening her prickly tone. "I'm sorry you have to work on Christmas Eve."

"Oh, I'm just doing as Christ would do. 'Whoever comes to me shall not hunger.'"

Dana sees the crucifix hanging from Grace's neck and has an internal allergic reaction; but she manages a smile on the outside before the waitress steps away and disappears into the kitchen.

This gives Dana a clear view now of that the old man at the counter. He's no longer hunched over his mug, but swiveled on his stool to face the family. Vacant eyes and a scraggly beard, he's full-on staring across the empty restaurant. Dana feels the urge to confront the man, but decides it's best not to engage.

"Can we help you?" Fiona shouts at the stranger. Her mother's daughter for sure.

"No." The man shakes his head. "And I can't help *you* if you don't leave that house." He swigs straight from his flask with a shaky hand, whiskey dribbling down his whiskers.

"I'm sorry?" Greg says.

"You don't know. . . do you?" The man slips from his stool, stumbling toward their table. "What happened out there at the Thornton house." He's close enough now for Dana to smell his whiskey breath. "The Candy Cain Killings."

Fiona smirks. "Was that the sequel to the Willy Wonka Massacre?"

The man pulls a Bible from his breast pocket, holding it up as he starts his sermon in the dimly lit diner. ". . .and I will be hidden from your presence; I will be a restless wanderer on this earth, and whoever finds me will—"

A slow clap resounds from the front door.

Dana's eyes snap toward the uniformed sheriff who's just entered. A bear of a man with a grin beneath his white mustache, now approaching the drunkard. "That's a fine sermon, Pastor Wendell. But these folks are looking for eggs and bacon, not fire and brimstone. So why don't you head on back across the street? I'll pick up your tab here and we'll chalk it up to a church donation."

"Sheriff." The sloppy pastor shakes his head. "These folks, they need to know—"

"Nobody needs to know a thing, other than it's Christmas Eve, and everybody deserves a little peace on Earth. Wouldn't you say, Pastor?" The sheriff's paw clamps down on the pastor's shoulder, sending the already wobbly man into a wider wobble.

Wendell nods before turning back to their table. "God help you."

He's quick to leave the diner now, and Dana watches

through the window as he scurries across the street and into the church for sanctuary.

"Sorry about that," the sheriff says. "The older he gets, the more Old Testament he preaches. I'm Sheriff Brock. You must be the renters."

"*The* renters?" Dana repeats.

"We don't get many visitors in our small town. That Lynette woman caused quite a stir when she swooped in and fixed up the Thornton house without consulting the community first. Some folks are wary of outsiders, that's all."

"I'm sorry," Fiona interrupts, "but are we just glossing right over the whole Candy Cain Killings bit? What was he talking about?"

"Nothing more than a local legend, I assure you," Brock says. "Like Santa Claus. You're old enough to know Santa's not real, right?"

"I'm old enough to know cops aren't friends." Fiona crosses her arms. Dana's own anti-establishment streak kicked in at around fifteen years old, back when punk was still punk. At twelve, her daughter has one hell of a head start.

"You folks are from Los Angeles, I take it?" Brock asks, not waiting for a confirmation. "I can understand the distrust. But I'm here to protect and serve, I assure you."

Greg trembles in the face of the law. "We're not trying to start any trouble."

When did her husband get so damn submissive? His weakness only emboldens Dana to ask the sheriff, point-blank: "What's the legend?"

Brock looks around at the table. "I'm afraid it's not really a story for children."

Fiona motions to the empty diner. "I don't see any children around here."

The sheriff adjusts his belt. Gun on one side, taser and pepper spray on the other. A lot of weaponry for a small-town cop.

"A family died in that house, ten years ago tomorrow. Husband and wife with two small children. A good family, churchgoing family. Used to go caroling through town every Christmas Eve. So, you can understand Pastor Wendell getting a little emotional on the anniversary."

"Who killed them?" Austin asks.

"*What* killed them was a fire. Just a tragic accident caused by faulty tree lights. But I guess some folks just don't know how to process a thing like that. Whispers in Sunday school snowballed into legend, and the children conjured up a boogeyman. Suddenly, it was Candy Cain who killed that family. Punished them for their sins. Like I said, it's nothing more than a cautionary tale dreamt up by a God-fearing community. But it sure keeps the little ones in line come Christmas time."

Dad shakes his head. "Lynette didn't mention anything about any of this."

Brock smirks. "I don't reckon 'local haunted house' looks very good on a rental listing."

Dana suddenly remembers the strange look on Lynette's face when she mentioned her brother "passing." She wishes she had pressed and asked more questions; but more than that, she wishes her husband had done his research.

"Listen." Brock digs into his shirt pocket. "I'm sure you folks won't have any trouble out there." He hands Greg a card. "But if you need anything at all, I'm just a few doors down Main Street here. Don't hesitate to holler, okay?"

"Right," Greg says. "Thank you, Sheriff Brock."

"Be seeing you all at Christmas morning service?" the lawman asks, resting his hands on his well-armed hips.

Fiona lets out a scoff. "Not a snowball's chance in—"

"We're not sure how long it will take to open the presents and everything," Greg interjects. "But we'll try our best to make it."

"Of course." Brock smiles at the kids. "I hope Santa brings you everything your little hearts desire."

He walks off as Grace emerges from the kitchen with a tray of food. "Oh, hey sheriff. Coffee to go?"

"Got a full thermos in the car, thank you, Grace. You just take good care of our visitors here, will you?"

"I sure will." Grace distributes the plates.

Dana looks down at her salad, smothered in so much oil, it might actually be flammable. Just like the house her husband rented for this wonderful family vacation.

"I'll call Lynette," Greg promises.

Dana doesn't respond because if she opens her mouth, nothing nice will come out.

It's a silent night in the diner after that.

CHAPTER FIVE

L ynette parks her Hyundai on the main road, out by the rusty mailbox that Rick was supposed to replace.

A few inches of snow have gathered on the long driveway as she trudges up toward the cottage. She probably could've parked in front of the house, but she doesn't want to risk getting caught. She's already been so patient, waiting in her car until she saw the family drive away. What if that diner was closed after all and they turned right back around? It's not worth taking chances, not with her first one.

She uses her spare key to enter the house, making sure to slip her snow boots off outside the door. She can't leave a trace that she was here, and she doesn't want to ruin those brand-new hardwood floors with water damage. Rick did a great job there; she'll give him that. She just can't believe he jetted before finishing the job. Serves her right for hiring cheap local labor.

No matter. She got what she needed out of him. Looking around at the cozy living room, she's thrilled to have her very own tourist trap.

Securing the deed had cost her a few small bribes to lawyers and judges, thanks to her idiot brother leaving behind years of back taxes. He and his lunatic wife were religious fanatics, doomsday preppers. Lynette's poor little nieces didn't stand a chance being born into that madness. The last time she saw the four of them was at a family barbecue where her brother hopped up on the picnic table and shouted about how everyone was going to hell for their sins.

Kind of funny when you think about it. He spent his whole life banishing people to hell only to be burned up in his own home. And if the stories were true, about what happened *before* the fire. . .

Lynette's just glad the fire fighters put out the flames before the whole house crumbled. The place was in terrible shape by the time she gained ownership, but she knew how to slap lipstick on a pig and turn a pretty profit.

Maybe it was a gamble, but gambling isn't an addiction like some folks say. It's a skill set, one that she honed at the craps table first before diving into the dot com boom. If you don't move fast and take chances, the world will leave you behind; and Lynette is done being left behind, by her family, by her shit ex-husband. She's an entrepreneur, building herself an empire, and her Bible-thumping brother can suck it from beyond the grave because this house is hers now.

No, it's not a gamble. It's an investment, and Lynette has plans for this rental property to pay off in more ways than one. The internet makes scamming easy, with more rental websites cropping up every day. It's a booming industry with little oversight.

All she has to do is greet every guest with a smile while casing their belongings, then sneak in when the family is out and pluck what she can without being too suspicious. If anybody complains or accuses Lynette of theft, she'll be all: "It's clearly stated in the rental agreement that I'm not responsible for any lost or stolen property. Are you sure you locked all the windows and doors?"

It's not like there's a Better Business Bureau for personal home rentals. Still, if she wants to attract new customers and keep her ads alive on those sites for more than one rental, she'll have to be careful with this first family. She can't go too overboard, just a little icing on the cake.

Lynette checks the presents beneath the tree first, but there are only two there marked for the kids. Sad for them, sad for her. But it's the parents' presents she's really after.

She sensed some tension there between the mister and the missus, which meant the nerdy little man had likely gotten his wife something special to smooth things over. Some kind of surprise, probably hidden upstairs, close to the bed so he can whip it out tonight in the hopes of getting laid. That's what Lynette's ex would've done. Always an angle.

Lynette slinks up the steps, stopping off in the bathroom first. No way that woman didn't bring some kind of prescription from La La Land. Sure enough, she finds a few orange bottles and plucks a Valium with a grin.

"Merry Christmas to me." She pops the pill before heading into the master bedroom.

It looks like the parents have already unpacked their bags, so she starts rummaging through the dresser. Tucked away in the sock drawer like a dirty magazine, she finds her holy grail.

A foot-long box wrapped with a little note attached.

For Dana. My North Star. Love you to the moon and back. Greg.

Gag.

Lynette eagerly tears through the wrapping paper, not noticing when the note flutters to the floor. She opens the box to find a gold necklace within, a diamond star pendant hanging from the chain.

"Tacky bastard," she says. This style definitely does not match his classy wife, so Lynette's probably doing them both a favor by stealing it.

She carries her find over to the window to examine the diamond under the daylight. Her own engagement ring turned out to be a fake, which is how she knows this one's real and can definitely be pawned for a hefty stack.

Her grin turns into a frown when her gaze falls from the necklace down through the window, to the truck parked behind the house.

Isn't that Rick's truck?

Creak.

Someone's moving up the steps.

"Rick? Is that you?" Lynette tucks the necklace back into the box and slides it into her blazer pocket before stepping out of the bedroom onto the landing.

No one there. She leans over the railing, looking down into the living room, but the house is empty below.

SLAM.

A door in the kids' room.

"Rick, stop screwing around."

Lynette rushes into the kids' bedroom and sees that the bathroom door she left open is now closed.

She tries to open it, but it's locked from the inside.

She twirls on her feet, back onto the landing, and heads into the master bedroom. When she opens the bathroom door on that side, she finds an empty bathroom.

The door on the other side is wide open now.

Someone's screwing with her.

She passes through the bathroom, and the door *SLAMS* behind her.

Her heart jumps into her throat. "Christ!"

Fingernails scrape against the wooden door as a soft voice whispers behind it: "Thou shalt not take the name of the Lord thy God in vain."

Lynette steps back. That's not Rick.

The door swings open, but Lynette's already running from the room, back out to the landing. Not fast enough.

Two open palms slam into her back like pistons. The force propels her against the railing, which knocks the wind out of her as she tumbles and twists over it.

For a split second, her vision is filled with the upside-down Christmas tree. A glittering green arrow pointing down, down, down until her head hits that nice hardwood floor with a weighted *thud*.

Her muscles spasm, but she can't move her body,

every limb useless. She can't even turn her head to look at the figure skipping down the staircase.

Dry-skinned hands wrap around Lynette's wrists, dragging her toward the basement door as her assailant begins to sing off-key.

"Deck the halls with boughs of holly. Fa, la, la, la, la, la, la, la, la."

Lynette is pulled down the steps, her head *thump-thump-thumping* against every wooden step into the darkness below. But she can't scream, can barely breathe. She's paralyzed as the figure pulls her all the way into a darkened corner, leaving her sprawled on the dirt floor.

"'Tis the season to be jolly. Fa, la, la, la, la, la, la, la, la."

Metal clanks against metal, but Lynette's blurry vision is stuck staring at the unfinished ceiling. Until a box cutter is held in front of her eyes. She's forced to watch as the blade is pushed out as long as it will go.

"Don we now our gay apparel. Fa, la, la, la, la, la, la, la, la."

A hand digs into Lynette's pocket, retrieving the jewelry box and opening it. The pretty gold necklace is dangled in her vision, diamond sparkling even in the dark.

A dull rage fills the disembodied voice, no longer singing.

"Not your present. Naughty girl."

Lynette understands now that she's being punished.

She wishes she could speak, reason with her killer.

Beg Candy Cain for mercy.

But her throat is paralyzed as the box cutter is raised

up high and plunged down out of sight. The blade pierces into Lynette's stomach, just below her rib cage, nicking bone on the way in. It's more shocking than painful, until that razor-thin metal slices down and carves her open like a Christmas turkey.

Eager fingers dig into the wound, prying her belly open wide to the deepest cold Lynette's ever felt. There's no mistaking the feeling of hands rooting around her organs, unboxing her insides as blood pools within.

"Troll the ancient yuletide carol. Fa, la, la, la, la, la, la, la, la."

Lynette feels a harsh tug before another object is held in front of her eyes.

A stretch of rope?

"Deck the halls with boughs of holly. . ."

No, not rope or boughs of holly.

Intestines.

"Fa, la, la, la, la, la, la, la, la."

CHAPTER SIX

G reg drives back to the house on thin ice, literally and figuratively. The weather's getting bad and Dana's hardly said a word since their encounter with the sheriff. He's so focused on his wife's mood that he doesn't even notice the parked car gathering snow by the mailbox as he turns the station wagon down the driveway.

But the night's not over yet. It's not too late to salvage this Christmas, to save his family. They've got this beautiful cottage all to themselves with nothing to do but spend time together.

As they walk up the porch, Fiona points her cane at a pair of tall rubber boots outside the front door. "Whose are these?"

Greg shrugs. "Must've been there when we got here."

"I didn't see them."

"Maybe Lynette left them for us."

"Because she's so thoughtful," Dana interjects before entering the house.

"Maybe they're Candy Cain's," Austin says, prodding his sister.

"Can we all try to put that behind us?" Greg asks, hanging up their coats.

"Honey," Dana starts, no honey in her tone. "You brought us to a house where a family died on Christmas morning. It's kind of hard to put that behind us on Christmas Eve."

"I told you, I'll call Lynette first thing in the morning. Maybe I can get us a discount."

"A *discount?* On that wad of cash you handed her like a *Sopranos* goon? Wake up, Greg. She fleeced us. Did you even read the rental agreement you signed?"

Greg doesn't answer, because no, he didn't.

Dana shakes her head. "God, you are such a pushover."

"I'd rather be a pushover than a cold—" Greg catches himself.

"Oh, just say it. You know you want to, so call me a bitch already."

Greg shakes his head, not falling for the trap. This was their new dynamic. Greg would walk on eggshells around his wife, fearful of saying or doing something to earn her spite. But that only kept him at a distance from her, leaving room for resentment to build in the space between. It wasn't always this way, which is how he knows it's still possible to get that spark back.

"Hey," Fiona shouts after Austin, who's slinking up the staircase. "Don't leave me down here with them." She starts to follow her brother up the steps.

"Where are you two going?" Greg motions for them to come back to the living room, forming an impromptu plan out of sheer desperation. "Come on, we're gonna open presents tonight. A special treat."

Austin lets out a sigh as he slips back down the steps, and Greg gathers everyone in front of the twinkling tree. Lynette had at least done a great job with that.

"Okay," he says to his unenthusiastic children. "So, rather than getting a bunch of junk you're just going to be bored of in a month, your mother and I decided to get you each one useful present this year."

Dana hands Fiona her present in its large, wrapped box. "Merry Christmas."

Fiona opens it to reveal a brand-new pair of forearm crutches. Even though the insurance didn't cover them, Greg splurged on the expensive multi-function ones with lots of adjustable features.

"This part folds down." Greg shows his daughter the release button. "So, if you want to adjust the height or use them without the forearm holds—"

"I told you I didn't want crutches," Fiona says.

"We know, sweetie." Dana puts a hand on Fiona's. "But Doctor Keating said that if we don't want the joint damage to affect your growth, you're going to need more support."

"Don't you think I know what I need?"

This is not the reaction Greg was hoping for. "Okay, well. When you're ready, you have them."

Fiona settles deeper into the couch and crosses her arms in front of her chest.

"Austin." Greg hands Austin the small box, hoping this one goes over better. "We think you're finally ready for this."

Austin's eyes light up as he tears the wrapping off. "A Blackberry?!"

Greg grins at Dana, but she's still avoiding his eyes.

"This is way nicer than the cell phone I asked for." Austin hugs Greg, a big win.

"That's because it's not just any phone,' Greg explains. "It's a work phone."

Austin cocks his head. "What?"

Dana leans forward. "Your father and I have been talking about it, and we think it's time you started earning your allowance outside of the house."

"I got you a job at my office," Greg says. "Just part time, to start. A couple of nights a week, plus some weekend hours. It's basic data entry, but it's a great start."

"We all need to start pulling our weight," Dana adds.

"Well, now that Fiona's got shiny new crutches," Austin says, "maybe she can pull her own weight too."

Fiona's quick with the comeback. "Hey, I'll enter data in circles around you."

"Austin," Dana says. "You keep saying you want more freedom. Earning your own money will do that for you."

"Can I even use this stupid thing for personal calls?" Austin holds up the Blackberry box.

"Who do you need to make personal calls to?" Greg asks. "You spend every waking minute with Mateo anyway."

Austin's face goes a shade of red Greg has never seen before as the words explode from his son's mouth. "I wish you'd just get a divorce already!"

Greg can hear the gentle hum of the Christmas lights as the air leaves the room. "What did you just say?"

"I said I wish you two would just get a divorce so we wouldn't all have to be miserable together."

"Go to your room!" Greg shouts, pointing up the stairs. He's never felt so angry with his son before.

"That's where I was trying to go before you dragged me back down here for the worst fucking Christmas ever!" Austin stomps up the steps, slamming the bedroom door behind him.

Fiona uses her cane to get up to her feet. "I'll go talk to him."

She starts toward the stairs as Greg points to her new crutches. "Don't you want to at least try your—"

Dana catches his eye, shaking her head with a *Don't push it* glare.

Greg sinks onto the couch next to his wife. The *D-word* has been silently hovering over them like a dark cloud, neither of them daring to speak it. But now that it's out in the open, it feels like the rain is bound to come pouring down on their heads.

"I do have a present for you," Greg says, "but it's up in the bedroom. It's not sex. I mean, we *can* have sex. We *should*, I just mean I actually got you something that—"

"What if he's right?" Dana asks, staring straight ahead at the sparkling tree.

Greg is desperate to say the right thing. He wants to comfort his wife, assure her that everything will be okay. But as he stares into a big red bulb on the tree, he sees an unhappy couple reflected back at him.

All he has to offer in this moment is the truth. "I don't know."

Dana swallows hard, clears her throat. "Right. I'm gonna take an Ambien and call it a night."

Greg lets her go, his gaze falling to the cold fireplace. He'd envisioned a Christmas Eve spent snuggled up with his wife in front of a roaring fire. Then upstairs to the bed beneath the starlit skylight, where he'd give her the necklace and remind her of their first date at Griffith Park Observatory. Cue passionate lovemaking.

Damn it, he was sure the listing said "working fireplace." Why would the big iron poker and shovel be here if it wasn't usable?

Maybe Lynette really had pulled a fast one on him. Maybe Greg really is a pushover.

Either way, Austin was right about one thing.

This is the worst fucking Christmas ever.

CHAPTER SEVEN

Fiona cracks the door open to the dark bedroom, finding the bottom bunk empty. She lays down on top of the sheets, resting her weary bones.

"I called top bunk," she says into the crack between the wall and the bed above.

There's no response, but she knows her brother isn't sleeping yet.

He finally replies. "I guess nobody's getting what they asked for today."

Despite the sass, it's still a moment of connection. Those are rare these days, and Fiona doesn't want to let it slip away. "I know it seems like Mom and Dad only focus on me sometimes. But they don't actually listen to me, either. You see that, right?"

"I know," he responds, exasperated.

"And I try, I really try to. . . need less. But it's hard, okay?"

"I know," he says again, a bit more compassion in his tone.

It gives her the courage to ask: "Do you really want them to get a divorce?"

It's not that Fiona hasn't thought about it too. Maybe even anticipated it, but she doesn't think she *wants* it. Or at least, she didn't think that she *might* want it until her brother spoke the words.

"I just wish things were easier," he says. "That's all."

Austin doesn't know how easy he has it. Fiona's own body has been trying to tear her apart since the day she was born. She's spent her whole life shuttling from one doctor to the next, being poked and prodded, trying one treatment after another. Her knees are throbbing white hot just from coming up those stairs, but she's not going to throw any of that in her brother's face right now.

"Who would we live with?" she asks. Her mind is running a mile a minute, trying to picture the rift it would cause in her young life. "Do you think we'd be separated?"

"Fiona, I really don't want to talk about it."

"But you're the one who brought it up. I'm just scared that if—"

Austin's feet swing over the bunk above as he climbs down the wooden ladder, clutching a pillow under this arm.

"Where are you going?" Fiona asks.

"I'm sleeping on the couch. Congratulations, you got your own room."

"I didn't—"

"You didn't ask for it, I know. You don't ask for anything, yet somehow, you get everything anyway."

He's already opened the door, halfway out, but Fiona's done being patient, can't let him get away with it.

"You're not nice, Austin." Her voice cracks as she says it, but it doesn't seem to lessen the impact. It stops him in his tracks long enough for Fiona to hammer it home. "You're a bad brother."

His head hangs for a moment, silhouetted by the light on the landing as he speaks over his shoulder. "You want to know the truth? I do think Mom and Dad will get a divorce. And it'll be because of you."

He steps out onto the landing and closes the door, leaving Fiona alone in the dark with his weighted words.

She won't cry. No, she will not cry.

That's what she tells herself as the pillow soaks up her tears.

CHAPTER EIGHT

The moment Austin closes the door, he regrets it.

That was way too harsh. Fiona just caught him off guard with that "bad brother" comment. Why couldn't she just call him an asshole or a dickhead? He could've easily shrugged those off and shut his mouth, but "bad brother?" That just felt too mean.

Too true.

Deep down, he knows that his parents' issues aren't Fiona's fault. She's carrying enough weight as it is, and she doesn't need her asshole brother piling on.

See, asshole fits just fine.

Austin turns back to the bedroom door, ready to open it and apologize, but he pauses when he hears a strange *thump* downstairs.

He peers over the railing to the living room below. The tree lights have been turned off, so it's just a big spiky shadow in an empty dark room.

"Dad?" He creeps down the stairs, peeks into the kitchen. Nobody's down here.

Austin shrugs off the sound, puts his pillow on the

couch and curls up with a blanket. He can apologize to his sister in the morning after everyone's had a good night's sleep.

But he doesn't think he can sleep with all that whispering coming from behind the basement door.

Who the hell is that?

Austin creeps over to the door, leans his ear against the wood.

It definitely sounds like a voice, but when he cracks the door open to listen, all's quiet down there in the dark.

He flips the light switch on, taking one rickety wooden step at a time. A plank near the bottom is busted almost all the way through, but he manages not to trip on it.

When his feet land on the earth below, the stench punches him in the face. It smells like that time Henry Franklin shit his pants in gym class and hid the dirty clothes in his locker. Coach Cran was not happy when he finally hunted down the source of the locker room death-stink.

Austin notices another staircase, this one made of stone, leading up to closed storm doors. The wind whistles sharply through the crack. Maybe that was the whispery sound he heard?

The further he moves from the lightbulb, the darker it gets.

But he can definitely make out wet footprints on those steps.

Someone tracked in snow from outside. Recently.

Austin spins back toward the stone columns scattered throughout the shallow space.

The whispers are clear now, coming from behind one of those pillars, though it's hard to say which one.

The real question is: *Which staircase should I bolt for?*

But for some reason, the one he asks aloud is the same dumb question every horror movie victim asks: "Who's there?"

As soon as the words leave his mouth, a body leaps out from behind a pillar.

Austin falls backwards to the damp earth as a chorus of voices scream: "Merry Christmas, motherfucker!"

Austin's eyes pierce through the dark, finally making out the face of his attacker.

"Mateo?"

Mateo smiles brightly, a Christmas wish in the flesh now reaching down to pull Austin to his feet. "Sorry for the 'motherfucker.' That was Val's idea."

Valerie reveals herself from behind a pillar, holding a very '90s camcorder as she grins. "It makes for a funnier video. That and you pissing yourself."

Austin checks his pants to make sure he hasn't actually pissed himself.

Ethan appears behind Valerie with his joker grin. "I'm telling you, it would've been funnier if we dressed up like ghosts or something."

"And how exactly do ghosts dress, Ethan?" Valerie asks.

Ethan puffs his inhaler with a shrug. "I don't know, like. . . old-timey and shit."

"I don't understand," Austin says. "You all came out here just to *Jackass* me?"

"We came to hang, man," Mateo says.

Valerie holds up the old camcorder. "We just found this on the shelf and improvised our surprise."

"You skipped town on such short notice," Mateo explains, "and we know how much you hate family time."

"How'd you even know where I was?" Austin asks.

"Your away message," Valerie says, paraphrasing it from memory. "*Staying at a cabin in the woods with my family and no internet. If I never come back, find my dead body at 152 Delilah Lane.* Pretty dramatic, Austin, even for AIM."

Austin cringes as Mateo knocks his shoulder. "I'm surprised you didn't add any MCR lyrics."

"Whatever." Austin shoves Mateo. They'd spent many nights driving around town together, blasting their favorite screamo band and thanking each other for the poison. Right now, he's just grateful their friendship doesn't seem to be ruined after all. "I can't believe all your parents let you leave on Christmas Eve."

"Hey," Ethan says, "we're not all gentiles, jerkoff."

"My family's in a food coma by five," Mateo explains. "So, we just waited for Val's mom to down her chardonnay nightcap, snatched the keys to the Benz and took off like Blitzen. Figured we'd have a few drinks, sleep 'em off, and be back in LA before it's time to unstuff the stockings."

Mateo has a habit of talking in Tarantino, which

most people find intolerable, but Austin just finds endearing.

"Speaking of the Benz," Valerie says, "we parked out by that other car on the main road and walked up the driveway, so I better not get a ticket." She stomps her fluffy boots on the ground. "Probably ruined my Uggs in the snow, but we didn't want your parents to see us."

"Wait, what other car?" Austin asks.

"Oh, there's a truck out back too," Ethan points out the little raised window, where tires are visible through the falling snow. "Did we miss a party or what?"

Austin's trying to process all this information when Mateo puts a beer in his hand.

"No," Mateo says. "We *brought* the party."

All questions and confusion melt away as Austin gazes at Mateo, who says, once more with feeling: "Merry Christmas, motherfucker."

"Can we please go upstairs?" Valerie asks, popping the top off a bottle of Smirnoff Ice. "It smells like literal death down here."

"Absolutely not," Austin says. "The upstairs hallway overlooks the living room. My parents will definitely wake up and freak out."

Ethan holds up a joint. "Well, who wants to hotbox a creepy old basement?"

"Me." Valerie moves toward Ethan. "I'm fucking stressed from that drive."

"Hey," Ethan asks, "what's the difference between Saint Nick and Santa Claus anyway?"

"I don't know, Ethan. They're both made up."

As those two crowd around the joint, Austin shakes

his head at Mateo. "I can't believe you came all the way out here."

Mateo swigs his beer with a grin. "Happy to see us?"

"Yes." Austin's only had a few sips of alcohol, but he's feeling bold. "I'm happy to see you."

"That reminds me." Mateo lowers his voice. "I feel like we really need to talk about the other night. Like, I don't want there to be any confusion or mixed signals. . ."

Austin knows what comes next. He's too mortified to hear it, so he jumps in to alleviate the awkwardness. "Dude, it was just a joke. Obviously. I mean, we were talking about the movie and I thought it'd be funny to like, pretend I was making a move, or whatever."

"Oh. Okay, yeah." Mateo scratches the back of his neck. "That makes sense. I guess I just thought maybe you—"

"Mateo," Valerie calls, ever the interrupter. She's holding a piece of mistletoe over her head. "Look what I found in one of these boxes."

Mateo walks over to his girlfriend. "We probably shouldn't be going through this stuff, Val."

Austin didn't think this day could get any worse, but here it is, getting worse.

"Oh, shut up and kiss me." Valerie takes a puff from the joint and pulls Mateo in for a kiss, exhaling smoke into his mouth. Mateo coughs and Valerie laughs.

"Austin?" Valerie offers the joint.

"Why not?" He chugs the rest of his beer and takes the joint from her.

"Attaboy!"

"I thought you didn't smoke," Mateo says.

"I'm sorry," Austin says, taking a tiny hit and trying to exhale as coolly as he can. "Am I giving you mixed signals?"

Valerie squints back and forth between the two boys. "You guys good?"

"Yo, this place is weeeird." Ethan is still rifling through the boxes on the shelves. "There's like a million cans of deviled ham in here. Was the family who lived here survivalists or something?"

"The family who lived here died here," Austin says, a little buzzed as he cracks another beer.

"Ha, ha." Valerie rolls her eyes.

"Seriously," Austin says to Valerie, but he's staring a Mateo. "It's not a joke."

"What's this?" Ethan points to a square wooden hatch in the middle floor.

Austin shrugs. "I don't know. The realtor lady said the whole basement was off limits."

Ethan puts a hand on the rusty ring in the center of the hatch door, about to give it a pull.

"Can everybody please stop touching things?" Austin asks.

Ethan throws his hands up. "Bah humbug, bro."

Valerie holds up the old camcorder. "Speaking of things we shouldn't be touching. How retro is this thing?"

"Eight-millimeter tape," Mateo notes. "Gonna be some classic grain on that footage."

Valerie grins at Austin. "Wanna see how scared you were?"

"I wasn't scared," Austin clarifies. "I was surprised. There's a difference."

"Well, let's see the difference then, shall we?" Valerie hits the clunky 'Rewind' button, flipping the viewer screen out so they can all see. The tape clicks as it hits the start, and Austin braces himself as Valerie presses 'Play'.

The screen fills with a Christmas tree.

This is not the basement footage.

"What is this?" Mateo asks.

"Huh," Valerie says. "I must've started recording in the middle of another tape."

"Oooh," Ethan hustles over to look. "Is it a sex tape?"

"No. . ." Austin says as the group crowds around the little screen to watch a home movie.

A home movie with a fateful date emblazoned in the corner of the screen. . .

CHAPTER NINE

Two young girls sit cross-legged in front of the Christmas tree. They're seven or eight years old, wearing matching red and white striped pajamas. One is all smiles and curly blonde hair, the other a mess of tangled black hair hanging over a sad disposition.

"Say Merry Christmas, girls!" a man says from behind the camera.

"Merry Christmas!" the blonde child says brightly.

"Very good, Abby." It's a woman's voice this time as the camera pans to reveal Mother, wearing a pure white gown. Her face is pale, eyes intensely wide. Mother's smile suddenly drops to anger. "Candace. When Father tells you to do something, you do it."

The camera pans back to the black-haired girl, zooming in on her gritted teeth. "Merry Christmas," she mumbles.

"Good," says Father from behind the camera. "Now. Who's ready to open presents?"

"Me, me, me!" Abby says, curls bobbing.

"Okay, Abby," Mother says. "You first."

Abby reaches for the biggest present and checks the tag. "To Abby. From Santa." She tears through the wrapping paper and unveils a brand-new tricycle. "Oh, I love it!"

"Let's see if it works!" Father says.

Abby hops on the little tricycle and rides in circles around the living room while Mother and Father cheer. Candace watches her sister, knees shaking with anticipation until Abby finally parks the bike and sits back down in front of the tree.

"Okay," Mother says. "It's your turn, Candace. I wonder if Santa got you that firetruck you asked for."

Candace reaches under the tree and checks the tag on the next present. "To Abby. From Santa."

She puts the present back, reaches for a different one.

"Ah, ah," Father says, finger wagging in front of the camera. "That counted as your turn, Candace. Now give your sister her present."

Candace hangs her head as she hands the present to Abby, who opens it with glee. "Oh, it's a Sleepy Sally Doll! Just like I wanted!" Abby squeezes the doll tight. Candace reaches her hand out to touch the doll's plush foot.

"Candace!" Mother shouts, and Candace's hand retracts. "Do not touch your sister's things. Now, try again."

Candace trembles as she reaches for another present. Checks the tag. Frowns.

"Read it," Father says, zooming in on his daughter's distraught face.

Candace doesn't speak.

"Read. The. Tag."

Camera zooms in even closer, the little girl's forlorn face filling the frame.

"To Abby. From Santa."

Camera zooms all the way out to catch Candace, once again, handing the present to her sister.

And the next one.

And the next one.

Every present is marked for Abby, and soon, all the gifts beneath the tree are gone.

Abby is surrounded by toys, touching one after the other, can't decide which to play with first.

Candace sulks in a sea of torn wrapping paper with no gifts to speak of.

"What's the matter, Candace?" Father asks. "Do you think maybe Santa forgot about you?"

Candace shrugs, helpless.

"Wait," Mother says, entering frame with a red stocking. "I just found this hanging from the fireplace."

Candace takes the stocking and smiles for the first time, her eyes going wide.

"Show it to the camera, Candace," Father says.

Candace turns the stocking to show the name CANDACE stitched in green lettering across the white fluffy top.

"Now," Mother says, "let's see what Santa brought you."

Candace reaches into the stocking and pulls out crumpled newspaper stuffing. Then more newspaper, then more. She finally digs deep into the bottom of the stocking, and her face falls as she reaches something.

She turns toward the camera, a deep sadness etched into her face.

"Go ahead," Father says, zooming out to frame the tree with Abby sitting beside her sister. A perfect Christmas tableau. "Show us what you got."

Candace pulls her hand out of the stocking to reveal a lump of black coal resting in her little palm.

"Oh no," Mother says. "Santa brought Candace a lump of coal. Abby, why do you think that is?"

Abby's face bunches up, the picture of innocence, yearning to please. "Because Candace is a naughty girl?"

"Because Candace is a naughty girl," Mother agrees. "Because she never stops fidgeting during Sunday service. Because she sang off-key when we went caroling last night. And Santa saw all of it."

"It's okay, Candace," Abby offers. "We can share my presents. Here, go for a ride on my tricycle."

Candace reaches for the handlebars.

"No!" Mother leaps into frame, pulling the bike from Candace and pointing a finger in the girl's face. "Not. Your. Present."

Candace cowers as Mother composes herself and sits back down on the couch.

"Abby," Father says behind the lens, zooming in on the girl's face. "Presents are not for sharing. You got the gifts that you deserve. And Candace got the gift that *she* deserves. Remember, Santa is a servant of Jesus Christ. If we question Santa, we question Jesus. And you don't want to question Jesus... Do you, Abby?"

Abby shakes her head, blonde curls swaying. "No, Father."

"Do *you* want to question Jesus, Candace?" Father asks.

Candace looks down at the lump of coal in her hand.

"Candace." Mother says. "Father asked you question."

The little girl's fist clenches around the hard black rock. Her empty eyes rise to look at her beautiful sister.

Candace's arm rears back and punches forward. The coal *crunches* Abby's nose as blood splatters the pine needles.

"Candace!" Mother screams, but the black-haired child is already climbing on top of her sister and slamming that rock down, over and over again into her sister's face. The sound of squelching flesh is louder than Abby's cries, which end abruptly as her face is reduced to a smear of red in the grainy video footage.

Mother drags Abby's limp body away from her monstrous sister. The camera drops to the ground, still pointed towards the tree as Father rushes into frame and grabs Candace by the shoulders.

"What is wrong with you?!"

Candace shrugs. "Ask Jesus."

She snags the string of lights from the tree and wraps them around her father's neck. Tugging tight, she pulls him to the ground, taking the tree down with them. Candace uses the string of lights like piano wire, sawing back and forth against Father's neck. The little glass bulbs shatter, sharp ends slicing his skin open as blood spouts from a nicked artery.

A spark flies from a broken bulb, catching on the brittle branches of the tree, fire blooming.

Mother screams and runs out of frame, footsteps stomping through the house.

Father's limp corpse rolls to the ground next to Abby. Blood pools on the floor beneath their mangled bodies.

Candace reaches for the camera, taking control of the video with a wicked grin.

"They're all my presents now."

She hops on her sister's tricycle and pedals into the kitchen, singing a Christmas carol.

"Away in a manger, no crib for a bed. . . The little Lord Jesus laid down His sweet head. . ."

A Christmas ham rests on a carving board atop the kitchen counter. Candace reaches up and grabs the two-pronged carving fork, silver and sharp in her grip.

"The stars in the sky looked down where he lay. . ."

She pedals out of the kitchen and around the first floor, searching as the tree fire grows bigger and brighter.

"Motheeeeer! Where are you? I haven't given you your Christmas present!"

Candace stops pedaling when she sees the basement door is cracked open.

"The little Lord Jesus asleep in the hay. . ."

She climbs off the tricycle and heads down the steps into the dark basement.

"Motheeeeer. . . Father and Abby are waiting for youuuu. . ."

Candace scans the space, finding nothing in the shadows, until she strolls over to the little square hatch in the floor.

"The cattle are lowing, the baby awakes. . ."

She pulls the lid open to find Mother huddled up like

a baby in the small space, barely enough room for her to fit inside.

"Silly Mother. You said this was *my* special room. Where you put me when I'm a naughty girl. Are you a naughty girl, Mother?"

"Candace... Please..." Mother is crying as she holds up a Bible. "What would Jesus do?"

A silent pause as the child considers her answer. "Weep."

Mother opens her mouth to protest or beg, but the sharp prongs of the carving fork shoot forward between her lips, piercing into the back of her throat.

"But little Lord Jesus, no crying He makes."

Candace gives one swift twist on the handle, turning the tines inside Mother's mouth. Blood gurgles over the steel as Mother's eyes go a bit wider.

Candace yanks the bloody fork out, continuing to film as her mother sputters and chokes on blood.

Camera zooms in.

Watching. Waiting.

When the stillness finally comes, Candace grabs her mother's hand and drags her body.

Out of the little floor cupboard.

Up the stairs.

Back to the Christmas tree, which is now blazing in a full-on bonfire, flames licking up to the ceiling.

Candace places her mother's corpse next to her father's and sister's. She puts the camera on the couch with a full view of the flaming tree and family in front of it.

Plucking bows from all the loose wrapping paper, she

places one on each of her family member's heads, turning their corpses into twisted little presents. She sits with them, finishing her Christmas carol as she watches the fire burn.

"Be near me, Lord Jesus, I ask Thee to stay,
Close by me forever, and love me, I pray."

Candace strokes her sister's pretty blonde hair, now stained red.

"Bless all the dear children in Thy tender care,
And take us to heaven, to live with Thee there."

CHAPTER TEN

The image of the fire fizzles and cuts to black.

The prank segment kicks in with whispers in the basement.

"Who's there?"

"Merry Christmas, motherfucker!"

Austin pauses the video on a frame of himself, terrified on the ground. He closes the camcorder screen and turns to his stunned friends.

"Yo," Ethan finally says, breaking the silence. "What the fuck did we just watch?"

Valerie is vibrating in her own skin. "That was a snuff film. We just watched a legit snuff film."

"Oh please." Mateo grabs the camcorder. "That was clearly just some amateur film student trying to make their own *Blair Witch Project*."

"Four years before *The Blair Witch Project*?" Ethan asks.

Mateo shrugs. "It's innovative, I'll give them that. And the gore effects looked pretty real."

"It *was* real," Austin says aloud, head spinning. "The Candy Cain Killings were real."

"The what?" Mateo says.

"There was this drunk pastor at the diner tonight, he tried to warn us. The family who lived here was killed on Christmas morning. The sheriff said they just died in the fire, but he was wrong. The legend is true." Austin is trying to catch everyone up while putting together the missing pieces on the fly. "Candace is Candy."

"Candy *Cain?*" Mateo spells it out. "Like, C-A-I-N?"

"Oh shit," Ethan says. "That one's in our book too. He got jealous and killed his brother. Just like that little girl in the video."

"Great." Valerie throws her hands in the air. "So, we can all agree that the psycho who killed her whole family earned a very cute nickname." She turns to Mateo. "I'm ready to leave now."

"It was ten years ago, Val. Besides, if this actually is the real deal. . ." Mateo taps the camcorder. "We just landed the movie rights."

Valerie crosses her arms. "Are you serious right now?"

"I think maybe I should wake up my parents," says Austin.

"I think that's a terrible idea," says Ethan.

"I think it's too late for that," says the voice at the top of the stairs.

All heads snap toward the open basement door, where a silhouetted figure grips a fireplace poker.

CHAPTER ELEVEN

D ana lowers the iron poker and comes down the steps. "What is going on down here?"

The Ambien had just barely kicked in when she'd heard the voices downstairs. Convinced there were intruders, she woke Greg and they armed themselves before opening the basement door.

"Come on, guys." Greg drops his fireplace shovel to the ground to pick up an empty beer can. "This is really not cool."

Dana would've preferred a burglar over a basement full of drunk teenagers. Way less complicated.

"Mrs. Werner." Valerie puts on her best princess voice, aiming for the matriarch. "We can explain."

"You better, Valerie. Because I'm the one who'll have to explain this to your mother." Dana had been on the receiving end of Ellen Lee's wino rage before, and she was not looking forward to it.

"I know you're mad," Austin says, grabbing an old camcorder from Mateo and holding it out to Greg. "But you have to watch this."

"Is that what this is about?" Dana asks. "You all came

here to make another one of Mateo's home movies?" Having seen their work before, she tried not to criticize the derivative dramas made by teenagers with no life experience; but now was not the time to support creative youth.

"I don't make home movies," Mateo insists. "I make cinema."

"Save it for Sundance. It's Christmas Eve, and you're all in big trouble."

"It's not our camera, Mom." Austin presses the 'Rewind' button. "Please, just watch it."

"Watch what?" says a small voice in the doorway above.

The group turns once again toward the top of the stairs, where Fiona stands on her forearm crutches.

Greg lights up. "Hey, how're they working?"

"Not the time, Greg." Dana rubs her temples.

"What's going on down there?" Fiona asks.

"Nothing," Dana calls back up to her. "Please go back to bed."

That's where Dana wants to go, to drift off to sleep and not have to deal with whatever it is she's about to deal with. Austin finally presses 'Play' and shoves the camera in front of her and Greg.

Dana squints at the image of two little girls sitting in front of a Christmas tree. Her eyes dart to the corner of the screen, where the date is branded in digital lettering. The basement suddenly feels ten degrees colder.

"Is this. . ." Greg asks.

"The family Sheriff Brock told us about," Austin says. "But there's more to the story."

Dana can hardly process what's unfolding on the screen, but she can't look away either. The emotional child abuse is enough to make her stomach churn, and she's definitely not prepared for the physical violence that follows. She keeps hoping that somehow this story will turn out differently than she knows it will, right up until the final frames.

Dana stares at the little girl, singing in front of the flaming Christmas tree with the family she just murdered.

"And take us to heaven, to live with Thee there."

"Jesus," Greg says, closing the screen.

"Happy birthday, right?" Ethan takes out a lighter to spark a joint.

Dana snatches it from him. "Really, Ethan?"

"Sorry," he shrugs. "Habit."

Dana's foggy brain is now actively fighting that Ambien she so desperately craved as she turns to Greg. "I'm not really sure where to begin."

She can see the gears turning in Greg's head as he makes his calculations. Usually, he'd get stuck there, frozen in indecision. But tonight, a Christmas miracle happens.

Dana's husband takes charge.

"Okay, here's what's going to happen. All you kids are staying here tonight. We'll call your parents, let them know you'll be home bright and early. In the meantime, I'm going to call the sheriff." He holds up the camcorder. "This is clearly evidence, and we don't want to tamper with a crime scene any more than we already have."

Dana is genuinely impressed. Maybe all those nights

she and Greg watched *CSI* reruns in silence until they fell asleep actually paid off.

"Did they not mention the murder in the rental listing?" Ethan asks. "Because people pay extra for that."

"Dad." Austin steps toward his father, taking the camcorder. "I really don't think we should stay here tonight."

"I know it was scary to see all that." Greg puts a hand on Austin's shoulder. Dana loves seeing him in Good Dad Mode. "But it happened a long time ago, okay? We're safe, I promise."

"But what if this place really is haunted? What if Candy Cain is still here?" Austin asks.

Dana interrupts, following Greg's lead. "Nobody's here except three underage kids whose parents are probably worried sick about them. Come on. Upstairs."

She shepherds everyone up the steps, where Fiona is waiting to ask: "Can somebody please catch me up?"

Greg pulls the phone from the receiver in the kitchen. He frowns, clicking the hook switch a few times. "Line's dead." He looks out the window at the falling snow. "Storm probably knocked it out."

Dana watches as he grabs his puffy coat from the hook.

"What are you doing?" she asks, following him to the door.

"It's a short drive to town. I'm gonna bring that tape to the sheriff and use his phone to call the kids' parents. Back in a flash, okay?"

"Okay, just. . ." Dana zips his coat up for him. "Take it slow out there."

"I will." Greg gives her a peck on the cheek before heading out the door.

"Where's Dad going?" Fiona asks.

"We found a video of the Candy Cain Killings," Austin explains.

"Oh, sick!" Fiona says. "Can I watch?"

She reaches for the camcorder, but Dana snatches it from Austin's grip.

"Absolutely not." Dana looks at the camcorder and realizes: "He forgot the damn tape."

She opens the front door to find a foot of snow already piled up on the ground below the porch. Good thing Lynette left those boots after all. Dana slides into them and rushes toward the station wagon just as the engine starts.

She bangs on the window, startling Greg. He rolls down the window, and she hands him the camcorder.

"Yeah." He blushes. "That would help." Greg puts the camcorder on the passenger seat, turns back to his wife.

"Drive safe, okay?" She glances over the roof, up the snowy driveway. "The roads look rough."

"He's wrong, you know," Greg says. "Austin."

"About Candy Cain still being here?"

"About us getting a divorce." Greg reaches out and squeezes Dana's hand. "We're going to be okay. All of us."

Maybe it's just the Ambien, but Dana has never loved her husband more than she does in this moment. She leans into the car and kisses him. Not just a peck on the lips, but a full-on sloppy-tongue make-out kiss.

Greg smiles like a schoolboy in the aftermath. "Hey, you saved Ethan's joint, right?"

"Oh, absolutely. We're gonna need it tonight."

They share a laugh. A rare occasion these days, and it fills her chest with a special warmth, even as her breath is visible in the cold.

"I love you," she says.

"I love you too."

Greg puts the car in drive, and Dana watches his tail-lights disappear into the white night.

She comes back inside and kicks the snow from her boots. "Okay. Mr. Werner's going to call your parents, so why don't we sort out where everybody's sleeping tonight?"

"Hey, Mrs. Werner?" Ethan's eyes are bloodshot as he asks: "Got anything to eat?"

Dana sighs. "Alright. Food first, then sleep. I hope you like leftover chicken fried steak."

Ethan's jaw hangs agape. "None of those words should go together, but I'm here for every one of them."

Dana corrals the kids into the kitchen; and for the first time in a long time, she misses her husband.

CHAPTER TWELVE

H alf of Greg's mind is in the station wagon, carefully navigating the snowy road toward town, but the other half is back at that house with his wife.

Despite all the setbacks, or maybe because of them, his plan actually worked. The spark was relit, he felt it in their kiss. In the grand scheme of things, one kiss might not be much, but it was a start. Enough to nurture back into a roaring flame.

Rolling down Main Street, it occurs to him that Nodland is the perfect name for such a sleepy town. Only a few side streets are visible with a smattering of homes. The church spire looms above as Greg follows the address on Brock's card, finding the little brick building just past the diner.

He hops out of the car, hoping it's not too late to call on the sheriff. It's never too late to call on a sheriff, right? That's what they're there for. He presses the intercom buzzer and peers through the glass window into the darkened office. It sure doesn't look like anybody's here.

"Brock here." The gruff voice rattles the old plastic speaker.

"Uh, hi, Sheriff. I'm sorry to bother you so late. This is Greg Werner, we met at the diner tonight? We're the family renting the old Thornton house?"

"Of course, I remember. Storm knock out your phone line?"

"I think so, yeah."

"That'll happen."

"Well, we found something in the house and. . . I think you're going to want to see this video, sir."

A gust of wind blows dusty snow across the sidewalk.

"Be down in five."

Down?

Greg takes a step back and looks up to the small window above the station, where a light flicks on. Less than five minutes later, the fluorescent lights sputter to life in the station. Brock's coming from another entrance, fully dressed in his uniform as he opens the front door just wide enough for Greg to squeeze through.

"Let's get you in out of that cold."

"Thank you." Greg welcomes the warmth inside, unzipping his coat. "You live above the station?"

"Never too far from duty. Coffee?"

"No, thank you." Greg holds up the camcorder. "I really just wanted to get this to you, maybe use your phone?"

"Well, I'm gonna need some coffee." Brock heads toward the coffee machine against the far wall. "Have a seat, make yourself comfortable."

Greg lowers into the chair in front of the desk. He plucks a picture frame and looks at a photo of Brock shaking hands with Pastor Wendell on the church altar. "Special occasion?"

"My confirmation ceremony." Brock scoops coffee grounds into the basket. "Every public servant in Nodland is elected by the church community. Divine duty, you might say." He snaps the basket shut, flips the switch.

Greg's never been one for organized religion, but he keeps that to himself. "Must be a good gig, policing a quiet town like this one."

"As Paul said to the Thessalonians: 'Aspire to live quietly, and to mind your own affairs, and to work with your hands.'" Brock looks down at his own big mitts, as if contemplating some past labor.

Greg feels himself getting impatient with the lawman who moves like molasses. "Would you like to see the video? While the coffee brews?"

"Sure. Let's see what you found." Brock takes the camcorder and sinks into the chair behind his desk. He presses 'Play' and watches. Greg can hear the awful sounds emanating from the speakers, but Brock doesn't react to any of it.

"Awful thing. Just tragic." Brock shuts the screen when the film is over.

"So, I guess maybe there's some truth to that legend?" Greg's trying his best to guide the sheriff toward some clarity, but the man is taking off on his own tangent.

"They were good Christians, they really were. Just

got a little stuck in the Book of Revelations, if you catch my drift."

"I'm afraid I'm not up to speed on my Bible studies." The only books Greg reads are about science and math and. . . reality.

"They were convinced a reckoning was coming," Brock continues. "The rapture. And when they had those twin girls, they took it as a sign. God had granted them two witnesses, just like that final book said. Only problem was they ended up with one angel and one devil. They tried their best, but Candace was a difficult child. You could see that yourself."

Greg chooses his words carefully. "I could see they abused her."

"I think, in their own way, they were just trying to make her good in the eyes of the Lord. Before it was too late."

"Well, I'd say it's too late now." The whole shape of this conversation feels off to Greg. He thinks about asking to use the phone again, but something tells him he should just hurry up and get back home to his family. "Anyway, I hope that video helps shed some light on the case." Greg gets to his feet. "I better get back before—"

"You know, I was the first officer on the scene, ten years ago." Brock has a wistful look in his eye. "The fire fighters put out the flames before the house could crumble to dust. I went in and found the charred remains in the wreckage. It was clear enough there'd been foul play before the fire."

The reason for Brock's utter lack of surprise suddenly clicks into place as Greg realizes aloud: ". . . You knew."

"Of course I knew. The way those three bodies had been slashed up and smashed up. . ." Brock shakes his head in disgust while Greg catches on one word.

"Three?"

"Candace was gone. I tried to keep it quiet, sell the softer version of the story I sold you and your family tonight. The one where everyone just died in the fire. But the damn M.E. leaked the truth to a local paper, and they ran with that *Candy Cain Killings* headline. Can't say I blame them. Familicide with a killer in the wind has a certain sensational quality to it."

Brock's eyes land on that photo of him with the pastor.

"But it's my personal mission, my God-given calling, to protect this town. To stop that kind of dark cloud from descending on my people. So, I stamped out the story before it could spread. It was too late to un-name the monster, but easy enough to spin it into a harmless local legend. You ever see *The Man Who Shot Liberty Valance*? 'When the legend becomes fact, print the legend.' I think it's John Wayne's best, personally."

The casual way this man is talking about a coverup has Greg ready to bolt for the door. But he has to ask: "Didn't you wonder what really happened to her?"

"I'd say it was pretty clear the girl wanted freedom, and that's what she got. Maybe she skipped town, started over. Maybe she crawled off to die in the woods, got eaten by wolves." Brock shrugs. "Either way, it didn't matter. Long as nobody went poking around that old house, finding things better left unfound. But some folks just don't know how to mind their own affairs."

There it is, that shift in the air. It's a primal feeling, something Greg's not usually in touch with, but there's no denying it any longer.

He's in danger.

The coffee machine sputters to a stop.

"Ya know. . ." Greg swallows hard. "I think I will have some coffee."

Brock starts to rise, but Greg moves first.

"Please, allow me." Greg goes to the coffee machine and starts taking inventory of the space. No weapons in sight. He pours himself a cup of coffee. "How do you take it?"

"Black with two sugars," Brock responds.

Greg's eyes dart toward a doorway, leading to a small dark kitchen. There'd be weapons in there for sure.

"I'm gonna get some milk, if you don't mind," Greg says.

"Afraid I'm all outta milk," Brock says. Greg turns, mugs in hand, to find Brock on his feet, gun in hand. "And you're all out of luck, pilgrim."

Greg stares down the barrel at this John Wayne wannabe. "Easy now, sheriff."

"I gave you a chance, back at the diner. Told you enough of the story, didn't I? Enough to make you leave? But you didn't listen."

"Are you really gonna shoot me?" Greg asks.

"It's not the cleanest kill," Brock admits, "but I'll be first on the scene again to tidy it all up. Way I see it, the best way to put a bow on this mess is to have us another fire. Let that house burn all the way down, just like it should have ten years ago. Another tragic accident.

Another unfortunate family. Newsworthy for a day, a week at most."

Brock points his gun at the camcorder. "But this video gets out? We'll never see the end of it. Especially not now, with the internet everywhere. The truth is harder to contain these days, and those godless media vultures will descend on Nodland. It'll be Helter Skelter, JonBonét, OJ-Goddamn-Simpson all over again. Pardon my language." He takes a deep breath. "Candy Cain will rise to fame, and then it won't just be her house. It'll be her town. And I won't stand for that."

"Destroy the video," Greg says. "I don't care. I'll take my family tonight, and we'll never mention this again." Hot coffee spills over the top of the trembling mugs, burning Greg's hands. "You have my word."

"See, I actually believe you. I believe that you're scared enough to know I'd come find you in Los Angeles if you ever broke your word. But what about your wife? I don't know that I'll have your son's word, either; and I sure as heck don't trust that daughter of yours to keep her trap shut. She's got some spunk in her for a cripple, don't she?"

Greg tenses at the mention of his family, at the slur against his daughter.

"Don't worry," Brock assures him. "I take no pleasure in cruelty. I'll make sure they don't feel a thin—"

Greg thrusts his arms forward, twisting the mugs outward. Coffee flies like two black jellyfish through the air, and a *bang* resounds in the small room. The contents of one mug fly over Brock's shoulder, splashing the wall behind him, but the other meets its target, directly in the sheriff's face.

Brock is screaming, pawing at the hot liquid scalding his skin. Greg should be seizing the moment to run, but he's looking down at the mug in his left hand. Or at least where the mug should be. It shattered to bits on the floor, leaving him gripping the cracked ceramic handle. It shattered because the bullet passed through it and into Greg's gut. His sweater blossoms red as his knees give out, falling face first.

"You son of a bitch!" Brock howls, no longer pardoning his language. "I'm gonna fucking kill you!"

Greg's only got one shot here, gripping the sharp mug handle beneath his slumped body as he taunts: "Come fight me like a man, cowboy."

Brock huffs around the desk to kick Greg in his bleeding stomach, rolling him onto his back. Greg wastes no time digging the ragged ceramic edges into Brock's thigh, yanking the mug handle down like a zipper to shred the muscle beneath. Blood gushes through polyester as Brock wails.

It's not much, but Greg hopes he at least slowed the son of a bitch down.

He hopes he's done something to help his family as the next bullet bursts through his broken heart.

CHAPTER THIRTEEN

Austin looks past the kitchen island, where Ethan forks leftovers into his face. He watches Mateo rub Valerie's shaking shoulders and can't help wishing he was on the receiving end of that comfort.

"You're an amazing cook, Mrs. W," Ethan says, taking another bite.

"I did not cook that thing," Mom says, digging into the freezer for another takeout container. "I forgot Dad ordered this ice cream to go. Anybody want some?"

Valerie nods. "That sounds nice."

Mom scoops some into a bowl for Mateo and Valerie to share, then brings one over to Austin and his sister. "Are you two okay?"

"I'm worried about Dad," Fiona says. Austin hates to admit it, but he is too.

"I know." Mom looks out the window at the falling snow. "But you know your father is as careful a driver as they come."

Austin knows that Dad's slow driving is one of the many things his parents fight about. But the driving conditions are not what's scaring him right now. "I can't stop thinking about that video."

"Yeah." Mom nods. "It was pretty graphic. But I think the worst part. . . was the mother." She looks down, hiding her eyes. "I know you two never met your grandmother, but she was a hard woman. And I told myself I'd never be like her. Then I had kids myself, and every day I worried. I worried you'd suffocate in your crib, get kidnapped on the walk to school or run over by a speeding car."

"Yikes, that's grim." Fiona takes a bite of ice cream.

"It is. And all that fear, I guess it ended up making me hard too. Parents do need to be tough, protective, because it's a scary world out there. But maybe I don't always have to be so cold."

"You're not cold," Fiona says.

"Yeah. I kinda am." Mom takes a bite of ice cream for herself. She never eats ice cream. "Look, I know things have been a little rocky lately. And maybe your father and I haven't been so sensitive to everyone's needs." She sighs. "Those were pretty shitty Christmas presents, huh?"

"Just the worst." Austin shakes his head, but he can't help laughing. His mother and sister laugh with him. "I mean, what were you guys thinking?"

"We were trying to let you know that we know you're not kids anymore. To encourage your. . . adulthood. Or something."

"But, Mom," Fiona says. "We *are* kids." There's a vulnerability in this plain admission that Austin doesn't often see from his sister.

"I know," Mom says, a quick reaction. Then she takes a moment to look at them both, like she's reappraising her own children with new eyes before affirming more thoughtfully: "I know. And you deserve better adults. We're trying the best we can, and maybe that's just not enough right now. But as soon as your dad gets back, you have my word. . . we'll try harder."

Austin feels a warm current pass through him, his sister, and his mother.

He knows she means it.

"Okay," Ethan says, interrupting the sweet moment. "I really appreciate the fine cuisine, but I'm about ready to call it a night. Valerie, Mateo? You ready to roll?"

"You're joking, right?" Valerie lowers a spoonful of ice cream from her lips. "I'm not driving home tonight."

"That was the plan, remember?" Ethan reminds her. "Sneak out, surprise party, and back before sunrise."

"Well," Mateo interjects, "I'd say stumbling upon a murder tape kinda threw a wrench into that plan."

"Exactly," Ethan says. "We found a murder tape in a murder house, and everyone's cool to just chill and wait to be murdered? Hell no. I've seen every *Reaper* movie, and the killer always comes back. I'm not about to wait for Candy Cain to come to town."

"Ethan." Valerie measures her words carefully. "Those are movies, you are high, and we are not leaving."

"Fine." Ethan tosses his plate into the sink and points out the window above it. "I'm gonna go scope out that truck and see if there are any keys in it."

"What truck?" Mom asks.

"You didn't know there was a truck behind the house?" Mateo asks.

"No, you all failed to mention it," Mom responds.

"It's been a bit hectic," Austin says. He'd already forgotten about that detail himself.

"Ethan," Mom says, catching him at the front door. "I really think you should stay here tonight. It's dark, and you've been smoking."

"I promise you, I'm sober as a peach, ma'am." Ethan points to his leg, which is bouncing furiously. "Hence the antsy anxiety. But if my parents find an empty bed in the morning, I'm dead. So, I'm gonna jet and not get dead, here or there."

"I can't allow it," Mom says, shaking her head.

"No offense, but you're not my mom." Ethan takes a puff from his inhaler. "You're way hotter."

Mom throws her hands up as Ethan heads out the door. "What's this truck he's talking about?"

"We saw it when we snuck through the basement doors," Valerie explains.

Mom goes to the window over the sink and cranes her neck to look outside. Her face falls when she sees it. "Shit."

"What?" Austin asks.

Mom darts from the window to pull the phone off the hook, smashing buttons.

"Mom, I think we've firmly established that the phone is dead. What's wrong?"

She slams the phone down and points out the window. "It says *Rick's Fix* on the side."

"Rick?" Fiona says. "Isn't that the guy the waitress

mentioned? The contractor who disappeared before finishing the job?"

"Okay. Question." Valerie raises the spoon in her hand. "Did you find out about this disappearance before or after you were warned about the murders and the fire? Because I'm having trouble keeping track of all the red flags you all just blew right past."

"Not helping, Valerie." Austin isn't in the mood for her attitude, even if she does have a fair point.

"Cool, so Ethan's right, then." Valerie shoves a bite of ice cream into her mouth to keep from crying. "We're all dead."

CHAPTER FOURTEEN

The moment Ethan steps out onto the porch, he sparks a fresh joint and takes a deep pull.

He's been told a million times by his doctor that he shouldn't smoke with asthma, but he doesn't care. In fact, he's actually found that if he smokes right after hitting the inhaler, the medicine helps the smoke go down smoother.

Or is it the other way around?

Either way, nothing else works for his anxiety, and his trembling leg is already slowing as he takes the second hit. He would never tell Mrs. Werner this, but he thinks he drives better stoned, too.

Ethan walks around the house to the truck out back and opens the driver's side door. He checks the visor, even though people only store keys there in old movies. Turns out he's not in a movie because the only thing that falls out of the visor is a coupon for free coffee at Nodland Diner.

He checks the center console next, but it's just random junk and a pack of mints. His mouth tastes pretty grimy from that chicken fried steak, so he pops a mint and pockets the rest.

Bang-bang-bang.

Ethan spins on his feet.

Mrs. Werner is slamming her fist on the kitchen window, shouting something through the glass, but Ethan can't hear a damn word she's saying. That woman could really use some weed.

"Chill!" he yells, walking over to the window. "No key! I'm coming back!"

He's right in front of the kitchen window now, and one word rings out loud and clear from Mrs. Werner's panicked face.

"Run!"

Before Ethan has time to match her panic, two hands wrap around his ankles. A firm yank sends him flopping backwards into the snow.

Ethan pushes up onto his elbows, looking toward the little basement window. Someone's pulling him inside with overgrown fingernails that dig into his jeans. He can't see a face as he kicks against the dark, but he feels ragged teeth sink into his calf. Ethan screams, his free leg flailing until his foot connects with what must be his attacker's head, because those eager hands finally let go.

Ethan scrambles to his feet, bitten leg bleeding. A figure crawls out of the little window like a spider, then stands tall with broad shoulders, and Ethan is frozen at the sight of her.

She looks about his age, but her face is obscured by the black hair hanging over her face. Her red and white striped pajamas are several sizes too small, the sleeves and pant legs busting at the seams halfway down her arms and legs, revealing splotchy skin beneath. One of those gnarled hands is gripping a large wrench as the girl huffs a visible breath into the cold night.

It's Candy fucking Cain.

The kitchen window behind her is now a tableau of screaming faces. Ethan wishes he could be safe inside with everyone else, but the monster stands between him and the house. He gives them all one last sad glance before turning and running for the trees.

Ethan's skipped every gym class with a doctor's note, but he's digging deep for any ounce of athleticism he can find now. His footsteps are slow in the snow, leg weak from punctured flesh.

The footsteps behind him are faster, so much faster.

Ethan turns to look over his shoulder and sees something straight out of a 3D horror movie.

A wrench hurtling straight at the screen. Only there's no screen here. Just Ethan's face.

The heavy metal clanks against his jaw, dislodging a tooth that tumbles down the back of his throat. Ethan swallows hard and falls backwards into the snow again.

He tries to sit up, face throbbing, but Candy Cain is already leaping, legs first. She lands on Ethan's chest like a deranged WWE star, straddling his torso and pinning him to the earth. He coughs, but his trusty inhaler is out of reach in his pocket. More shattered teeth come loose, and he swallows them down like vitamins with a gargle of blood.

Candy leans down, inches from Ethan's face, and he wants to offer her a mint because her breath is putrid as she starts to sing.

"Angels we have heard on high. . ."

She punches into the snow beside Ethan's head, grabs a handful and mashes it into a snowball.

He opens his mouth to scream, but Candy slams the snowball into it.

"Sweetly singing o'er the plains. . ."

Ethan gasps for breath, choking on cold ice, but Candy's already forcing another snowball down his throat.

"And the mountains in reply. . ."

Candy makes one more snowball, forcing it down his gullet again. That's when the vomit comes, chunks of chicken fried steak rushing up to escape, but it's got nowhere to go.

Candy's shoveling with both hands now, burying Ethan's face with snow. His face goes numb and his throat clogs as the ice melts into liquid, sliding into his lungs. He's not sure if he's choking or drowning or both, but he's painfully aware that he's dying as his arms and legs flail under the weight of the caroling killer.

"Echoing their joyous strains. . ."

Ethan's limbs give their last spasm, and he'll never need a doctor's note again.

Candy Cain climbs off her fresh kill.

"Glooooria. . ."

She admires the glorious snow angel the boy made with his funny little twitching.

"In excelsis Deo."

Candy turns toward the house, where more warm presents await.

CHAPTER FIFTEEN

Fiona stares out the kitchen window, her crutches going wobbly as the blood rushes to her head.

"What just happened?" she finally verbalizes.

It was hard to see everything from her vantage point, but she's pretty sure that someone just crawled out of the basement window, and chased Ethan into the distance, and jumped on top of him, and oh God, did she kill him?

The girl in red and white pajamas turns away from Ethan's motionless body now, toward her audience in the kitchen.

Mom turns to face the kids. "We have to get out of here. Now."

"Ethan's dead, isn't he?" Valerie says, voice rattling with shock.

"We don't have a car," Austin says. "And the truck clearly isn't an option."

"She killed him, didn't she?" Valerie again.

"We don't know anything for sure, Val," Mateo says, clearly trying to comfort himself.

"Yes, we fucking do," Valerie snaps. "That was her, the girl from the video, all grown up. That psycho just hunted our friend down right in front of us, and we're all next."

"Your car." Mateo changes the subject. "It's not too far. We can make a run for it."

"Speak for yourself." Fiona shrugs on her crutches. She hates being the squeaky wheel.

"Fuck that!" Valerie squeaks much louder. "I'm not going out there!"

"Then give me your keys and I'll make a run for it." Mateo puts out a hand.

Austin reaches out to pull Mateo's hand down. "Mateo, no."

"We stay together," Mom says. She herds them all away from the kitchen window toward the front of the house. "Town's not far. Your father will be back any minute with the car."

"So, we just wait?" Austin asks.

"Weapons," Fiona says, video game instincts kicking in. "We need weapons." She plays a lot of Warcraft online and has assembled a reliable team of friends to campaign with. They're the only real friends she has, outside of Molly. But looking around at Mom, Austin, Mateo, and Valerie, she feels a little less confident in their abilities to defend against a siege. Either way, they don't stand a chance if they don't arm themselves quickly.

"Look!" Mateo points, rushing to the front window.

Headlights pierce through the glass with the sound of a car approaching.

"Oh, thank God." Mom puts a hand on the door handle as everyone crowds around the front window.

"Wait," Fiona says. "Candy Cain's still out there."

The name sends a chill through the room. They all know what they saw, *who* they saw, but hearing it out loud just feels too crazy.

When the headlights cut out, the familiar shape of the family station wagon is visible through the snowfall.

"It's Dad," Austin says. "We have to warn him."

Mom manages to pull the front window open and shout through the screen. "Greg! Greg, hurry, it's not safe out there!"

They all watch as the car door opens, and Sheriff Brock gets out from behind the wheel.

"Why is the sheriff driving our car?" Fiona asks, gut sinking. "And where's Dad?"

The sheriff opens the back door to lift a limp body out, and Fiona recognizes the puffy coat immediately. Brock drapes Dad's arm around his shoulder, carrying him toward the house.

"A little help!" Brock calls from under the weight.

"Oh my God, Greg!" Mom rushes out the door and down the porch steps. She puts Dad's other arm around her shoulder and helps Brock carry him across the threshold into the house.

"What happened?" Fiona asks.

"We got into a little accident on the way here." Brock's leg is bleeding from a deep cut, his face inflamed pink.

It was hard to see through the snow, but the car didn't look banged up to Fiona. So, what kind of accident was he talking about, and more importantly: "Why didn't you go to the hospital?"

Brock responds by roughly releasing Dad's body, which collapses against Mom like a sack of bricks, knocking her to the floor under the weight.

"Mom!" Fiona lurches toward her mother.

"Not the best cover, I know," Brock says. "But that's all the time I needed."

He tosses the camcorder at Austin, who catches it instinctively, confused as the sheriff casually strolls back out and closes the front door behind him.

It's all happening too fast to process as Mateo finally says out loud: "All the time he needed for what?"

"Greg?" Mom is checking Dad's pulse, prying his eyelids open.

"Mom. . ." Fiona points to the bottom of Dad's puffy coat, leaking with blood.

Mom unzips the coat, and Fiona is instantly reminded that she's not in some bloodless fantasy video game with orcs and axes. The darkest red has blossomed around two gunshot wounds in her father's chest.

Everyone realizes it all at once, but it's Fiona who actually says it: "Dad's dead."

Austin rushes to the door and tries to open it, but it barely pulls an inch before snapping shut again.

Fiona looks out the window to see that Brock has just finished tying a bungee cord around the knob, securing the other end around the porch post for tension. He's trapped them in the house.

The sheriff gives Fiona a wink before heading to his car.

Cortisol spikes in her system, just like the shot the doctor gives her to ease the arthritis. Only this is all natural, pure fear.

Her mother is weeping on the ground with her father's corpse, and Fiona's trying to do what she does best.

Compartmentalize the pain.

But a little voice in her head is saying that it doesn't matter anyway.

They'll be joining Dad soon.

CHAPTER SIXTEEN

Brock grits his teeth as he limps toward the car, leg still bleeding from that sneaky bastard's cheap shot.

"Your old man put up a fight," he calls over his shoulder toward the house. "I'll give him that."

He pops the station wagon trunk, finding the red can of gasoline he'd moved there from his own cruiser. He always keeps it full in case of an emergency, and this was indeed an emergency.

An emergency cleanup.

As he trudges back to the house, Brock thinks of all the citizens of Nodland sleeping soundly in their beds on Christmas Eve. They have no idea the lengths he goes to serve and protect them; but he does it anyway. A thankless servant, just like Christ himself.

Arriving on the wooden porch, he walks backwards along the boards, gas can tilted to douse the whole thing. But too much weight on his injured leg sends his boot slipping on the wet wood, and he falls flat on his back.

Brock curses to himself, can't wait to be done with this mess. Thankfully, nobody inside saw the embarrassing display. They're too busy screaming and crying as he climbs back to his feet and calls through the window screen.

"You folks should've just stayed in the city."

There are more bodies inside than he met at the diner, but it doesn't matter. They all came from the same heathen hellhole called Los Angeles.

City of Angels, my ass, he thinks.

He would die before letting Nodland go rampant with crime and decay, lawlessness and sin. All it takes is one bad news story, one infamous crime to open the floodgates. It almost consumed them ten years ago, but Brock handled it, like he always does. He overdosed that loose-lipped M.E. on fentanyl and, wouldn't you know it, the paper printed a retraction on account of the unreliable source.

There was no Candy Cain, no violent murders in Nodland.

A tragic fire, that was all.

"He's gonna burn us alive," a young girl says inside now. "The fucking sheriff is gonna burn us all alive."

"That's right," he says. "A cleansing by fire, just like the good book says."

He needs to keep Nodland clean and pure. God's chosen people mustn't be tainted by outsiders.

Brock pats his pants pocket but finds it empty. He doesn't see the Zippo on the porch where he fell, so it must've slipped out in the car. He draws his gun instead, sending a clear message to the little girl on crutches still glaring at him through the grey mesh screen.

"Now, I know you ain't running nowhere, little lady.

But you best tell your family to stay put too. Because anyone who tries to escape is gonna find themselves shot like fish swimming out of a barrel."

Brock aims at her head, does a dramatic kickback motion like he's just pulled the trigger.

She doesn't flinch, looks past him now, into the tree line. Poor thing's gone catatonic.

He limps back to station wagon, checks the driver's seat and finds his trusty Zippo, emblazoned with that good old American flag. He's feeling damn tired by the time he gets back to the bottom of those porch steps.

The Zippo's metal top clicks open, and Brock's ready to light it up and finish the job.

"Wait," the cripple girl says. "If you're gonna kill us all, at least tell us why."

Brock sighs. He doesn't owe her an explanation, but he doesn't get to boast often. The cost of being a silent guardian.

"I already got into it with your daddy, so you're getting the CliffsNotes. When Candy Cain killed her family, she nearly killed this town too." He flicks his thumb over the wheel, sparking the flame bright. "It's time to put the legend to bed."

It could just be the window screen distorting his vision, but Brock swears he sees that little girl smiling as she says: "Why don't you tell the legend to her face?"

"What are you on about?"

She's definitely smiling now. "That's all the time I needed."

Brock senses it, a presence behind him as a little voice speaks over his shoulder: "So many toys."

There's a tug on his belt and he spins around to face the tugger. Brock swears he's looking upon a miracle.

Candy Cain herself standing before him, risen from the ashes like Jesus from the tomb.

He can't find his own words, so it's verse that falls from his lips: "And the dead will be raised imperishable."

This miracle of resurrection is the last thing he sees before Candy raises the pepper spray and presses down on the nozzle.

A blast of spicy liquid flushes Brock's eyelids open, and he collapses to his knees, dropping the Zippo in the snow. She grabs him by his thinning hair, holding him in place as the spraying continues. Brock screams, swears his eyeballs are melting right into his skull as he pulls the gun from his belt and swings it forward.

Candy's grip releases and there's a bustling of movement in the snow as Brock fires wildly. He hears bullets *ping* and *pang* off the station wagon until the gun *click-clicks* empty.

Did he hit her?

If he did, it doesn't stop her from singing.

"God rest ye merry, gentlemen, let nothing you dismay."

Brock can't see a damn thing now as he starts to crawl away on his stomach. He feels the tug at his belt once more.

That'd be the taser.

"Remember Christ our Savior was born on Christmas Day."

But Christ won't save Brock from what comes next. A mechanical *pop*, then two sharp pinches in his back. Those little metal hooks cling to his flesh, followed swiftly by 240 volts of electricity, surging into his muscles.

The lightning scrambles his brain, thoughts bouncing around like popcorn in his head, but one of those thoughts rings clear and bright:

Oh God, the gasoline.

It's soaking the back of his uniform from that stupid fall, making the polyester combustible; and combust it does, because the next thing Brock experiences is hell on Earth.

He doesn't full-on engulf in flames, but his back turns into a flaming grill on the Fourth of July as he thrashes face down in the snow. Even over the sound of his own screaming, he can hear the engine starting.

Brock roars back at the machine, helpless. He can't see it, but he knows what comes next. He just keeps crawling through the cold snow, his back a raging hellfire.

The front wheel skims the inside of his legs before slowly crunching up over his pelvis.

God, he wishes she'd just floor it and get it over with, but the car rolls slowly up his spine, *crack-crack-crack*ing every vertebra like a two-ton chiropractor.

All the while his insides are pushing, sliding up, up, up toward his head. He's a tube of toothpaste being squeezed until chunky red innards come oozing outward from his mouth, his nose; and there go his long-suffering eyes, popping loose from his skull.

The car door opens and Candy Cain hops out.

The flames on Brock's back are licking up the tire, into the engine.

She bends down, wraps her hands around his head. It's nice and loose from all the bone cracking and tendon tearing. Comes off in one firm tug, easy as a bow taped to wrapping paper.

She carries her dripping present toward the house, admiring the new trellis full of dead flowers.

Everything dies. Even pretty things.

Candy doesn't flinch when the *boom* comes next.

CHAPTER SEVENTEEN

A hot gust blasts through the window screen when the family station wagon explodes.

Austin's eyes water, staring at the hunk of fiery debris when he realizes Candy Cain has already disappeared into the night again. He turns back to the group with visions of carving knives dancing in his head.

"Fiona was right. We need to arm ourselves."

Everyone seems to agree as they shake out of freeze mode and into fight, rushing back into the kitchen. They pull out drawers and scramble to find any weapons they can. Unfortunately, Lynette did a terrible job of stocking the rental with the bare IKEA essentials. Austin just witnessed that girl rip a grown man's head off with her bare hands. No way is he going up against her with a green plastic spatula.

He slides a big kitchen knife from the block and turns to his sister. "Stay close to me, okay?"

"Grab me two steak knives," Fiona says. She clutches the smaller knife handles against the grips of her forearm crutches, blades pointed out like the horns of a bull.

His sister can clearly handle herself, but his mom is still staring vacantly back into the living room at her dead husband.

"Mom?" Austin steps into her line of sight, blocking the view. "Remember what you said, about trying harder?" Austin places the kitchen knife in his mother's hand, wrapping her fingers around it and squeezing tight. "It's time to try harder. We need you. Now."

Mom visibly swallows a lump in her throat, and Austin knows she's sending that fear somewhere deep into her gut, away from her nodding head as she says, "I'm here."

"Good." He turns back to see Mateo wielding a giant butcher's knife and Valerie dragging a heavy cast iron skillet off the stove.

"Are you sure you don't want something sharper?" Mateo asks.

"Absolutely not." Valerie shakes her head. "We don't know what we're dealing with. She could be a zombie, and stabbing doesn't kill zombies." She lifts the black pan by its grippy rubber handle. "But one swing to the skull with this will stop anything in its tracks."

Austin shakes his head. "She's not a zombie, Valerie."

"How do you know, Austin?"

"Because zombies aren't real." He doesn't actually know that, doesn't feel like he knows anything anymore. "And even if they *are* real, I'm pretty sure zombies don't grow up. I think Candy survived that fire somehow. Did you see what she was wearing? The same pajamas from the video."

A blur of red and white whistles past the kitchen window, and Valerie shrieks.

"Okay." Mom finally takes charge, snapping the curtain closed. "We're too exposed down here. Everyone upstairs. Let's go."

They scurry up the stairs, crowding into the master bedroom. It does feel safer, but Fiona asks the question on everybody's mind: "What do we do now?"

Austin darts to the window. He looks down to see the storm doors to the basement and the truck sitting beside them. "Rick's body has to be in this house somewhere, and I'm betting his keys are still on him."

"So, your plan is to go looking for dead fucking bodies?" Valerie asks.

"It's the closest car and our best chance of getting out of here," Austin says. "Unless you're ready to make a run for the road."

Valerie groans. "Please tell me somebody has a better idea."

All heads turn toward the only adult in the room. But Mom is standing by the dresser, reading some kind of note she just plucked from the floor.

"Mom?" Fiona asks.

Mom wipes her tears and tucks the note into her pocket, turning to the kids with welcome authority. "There are two ways into this room. Austin, Mateo. Help me move this dresser."

The three work together to push the heavy wooden dresser in front of the hallway door. Mom drags the wooden chair from the corner and jams it under the bathroom door handle to seal the other entrance.

"Someone must have heard that explosion, they'll see the smoke," she says. "We just have to wait it out. If she tries to get in, there's only one of her and four of us."

"Four of us *left*." The heavy pan trembles in Valerie's hand. "We shouldn't even be here. I should be home in my warm bed watching *Love Actually*. God damn you, Mateo."

"God damn *me*?" Mateo says.

"You just had to drag us out here to meet up with your secret crush, didn't you?"

Austin's heart sinks.

Mateo fumbles for words, finding a single unconvincing one. "What?"

"Oh, come on," Valerie says. "I'm not an idiot, even if you treat me like one. I know you two have a thing for each other. Everybody knows."

"A thing?" Austin feels the blood rush into his cheeks. "We aren't even. . . There's nothing to know."

"*I* know." Fiona shrugs.

"Yeah, honey," Mom chimes in, "It's pretty obvious, and very sweet."

Austin doesn't know what to say to them, so he turns to Mateo instead. "I mean. . . do you? Have a crush on me?"

Mateo looks down at the floor. "I did drag everyone out here with a half-assed plan just to see you. So, maybe, yeah. I kinda have a crush on you."

"Oh." Austin can't help smiling. "Cool. Me too."

Mateo grins back. "Cool."

Valerie interrupts the moment. "What's not cool is totally using me to come out here."

"You're right," Mateo admits. "I'm sorry, Val. That was fucked up. You don't deserve to be treated that way."

Austin speaks up. "I guess it just took us a little longer than everybody else to realize." This is not how he imagined this conversation would unfold, but relief swells in his chest as he looks around at his family and friends, all so accepting.

"It's fine." Valerie shrugs. "You two will make a very cute couple."

"Guys?" Fiona interjects.

"I mean, if we actually get out of here alive."

"Guys!" Fiona shouts.

"What?" Austin asks.

"Did you hear that?"

Austin can barely make out the sound.

A faint whistling.

"I think she's in the house," Fiona whispers.

CHAPTER EIGHTEEN

Valerie's grip tightens on the pan handle. She is *so* not ready for this. "Where's it coming from?"

Mrs. Werner leans her ear against the bathroom door first, then the bedroom door. She shakes her head. "Not there."

"Wait," Valerie says as the whistling gets louder. "I know this song."

She's been spending every afternoon at the mall a mile from school because her mom's too busy (or day drunk) to pick her up. Valerie doesn't mind the shopping sprees, but lately the Christmas music on repeat has been driving her nuts. The lyrics are ingrained in her at this point as she sings along to the tune in her head: *Ho, ho, ho, who wouldn't go? Ho, ho, ho, who wouldn't go?*

Mrs. Werner is looking at that note again. "My North Star. . . Oh God. The skylight."

Valerie's face falls as she hears the whistling directly above now. Her eyes move up to the ceiling.

To the skylight above the bed.

The lyrics spill from her mouth: "Up on the housetop, click, click, click. . ."

Crash.

Glass rains down from above as a basketball bounces off the bed and *thumps* to the floor at Valerie's feet.

No, not a basketball. It's Sheriff Brock's severed head. Stringy red things hang from his torn neck and ooze out his mouth.

"Run!" Mrs. Werner pulls the chair from under the bathroom door handle and guides everyone through.

But Valerie's too slow. Candy Cain drops down after the severed head, landing softly on the mattress with a giggle. The pajama-clad killer hops off the bed with her back to Valerie, lurching toward the bathroom door, where everyone is huddled inside.

Valerie rears back that heavy pan, rushing forward to throw an uneasy swing—

Thunk.

It barely grazes the back of Candy's head, but it's enough to send the little freak flopping face-first to the floor.

The wide-eyed group in the bathroom stares in awe as Valerie huffs.

"I told you. Blunt force trauma, bitches." She steps toward them. "Now, let's get the fuck out of here before—"

Candy leaps to her feet and rams her shoulder into Valerie's chest.

Valerie stumbles back across the room, still clutching the pan, which throws her off balance like an amateur shot-putter. Her pan hand crashes through the window, glass shattering and cutting her arm as the skillet drops out of the window. She winces, clutching her bloody forearm, but that doesn't stop her from taunting the monster.

"Come and get me, Candy Cunt."

Candy grunts, broad shoulders swaying as she stalks toward her prey like a cheetah.

Valerie's had enough knock-down drag-out fights in the school cafeteria to know that she can handle a girl this size with her bare hands.

Probably.

Right now, she's just praying Mateo hits his mark as he darts out of the bathroom, swinging the butcher's knife. The blade nicks Candy's shoulder, slicing a sliver of flesh to the floor with a *splat*.

Candy throws an elbow into Mateo's face, sending him stumbling backward into Austin's arms.

Valerie's grateful for the attempt, but knows Mateo is exactly where he should be right now.

"Cute couple," she says once more, just in case it's the last thing she'll ever get to tell them.

Candy slams the door on the group and jams the chair back under the handle.

The bell's been rung, and fight night begins.

Valerie's cornered against the broken window as she lifts her fists in front of her face. The gash on her arm isn't dripping so much as it is flowing like a soda fountain down her elbow.

She's losing a lot of blood, fast, as she grits her teeth at the oncoming killer.

The bathroom door is splintering wood as the butcher's knife hacks into it from the other side. Mateo's still trying, but it's too little too late.

Valerie goes woozy as her arms drop to her sides, too heavy to hold up. If she can't hit with her fists, she'll at least use her words. She peers through the black hair that hangs over Candy Cain's face. This girl might not be a zombie, but she sure could use a new skincare routine.

"God, you really are ugly. No wonder your parents hated you."

No reaction.

Valerie wobbles on her feet, blood pooling around her Uggs. Her eyelids flutter as she glances at the bed and thinks about how nice it would be to take a little nap right now.

Candy continues her deranged caroling as she steps an inch from Valerie's face.

"Give her a dolly that laughs and cries."

A finger extends to wipe the tears from under Valerie's eyes, the ragged nail scratching the skin of her cheeks. Bitch needs a manicure too.

"One that can open and shut its eyes."

Two fingers drag down Valerie's eyelids, closing them like a Sleepy Sally doll.

Yes. Just let her sleep.

Candy's palm clutches Valerie's face. It's a gentle shove, but it's enough.

Valerie's feet fly out from under her, body snapping backwards and catching on the windowsill.

Her eyes shoot wide open as she looks down at the jagged glass piercing up through her stomach. Too weak to hold herself up, Valerie lets her body go slack, hanging from broken glass by shredded guts.

She's seeing outside now, the truck and the basement doors below. As her limbs twitch, she can feel her severed insides slowly separating, and all she wants in this moment is for the pain to end.

To fall into soft snow and sleep.

CHAPTER NINETEEN

Mateo stops hacking at the door to peer through the ragged hole he made in the wood.

He sees Valerie bent backwards over the broken window, shards of glass protruding from her stomach.

Mateo screams her name, utterly helpless.

Candy Cain turns to look through the hole, into Mateo's eyes. She bends down and picks up Valerie's legs, tucking them under her armpits while facing the bathroom door.

Still singing.

"Down through the chimney with lots of toys. . ."

Candy leaps forward, giving a full-bodied yank that tears Valerie's legs from her torso, which topples out of the window. Mateo gags at the sight of Candy swinging Valerie's detached legs around in circles, blood splattering the walls.

"All for the little ones, Christmas joys!"

She releases the legs, which soar out the window to join Valerie's torso below.

Mateo starts hacking at the door again, but Austin pulls him back.

"Mateo. We have to go."

"I should've saved her," Mateo says, guilt washing over him.

"There's nothing you could've—"

A candy-cane-striped arm shoots through the splintered wood and grabs Mateo's hair. Austin swipes his knife against the hand, drawing blood before it retreats back into the hole with a hiss.

"Let's go!" Mrs. Werner pulls them out the other bathroom door, slamming it closed. They hurry from the kids' room out to the landing, closing that door too.

"Fiona," Austin says. "On my back."

Mrs. Werner carries the crutches, but Fiona's still clutching those steak knives as she wraps her arms around her brother's neck.

"Please be careful with those," Austin says.

"You guys go first." Mateo grips the butcher's knife tight, facing the kids' bedroom door as the rest of the group slips down the stairs.

He let Valerie die, but he won't mess up again. As soon as Candy opens this door, he'll be waiting to—

Slam.

The master bedroom door flies open down the hall. Mateo spins toward it as Candy Cain steps out.

"Go, go, go!" Mateo shouts over his shoulder, raising the wide blade high.

He's ready for Candy to charge straight down the open hallway at him. But she doesn't. She takes a few steps back and sprints diagonally toward the banister, leaping over it.

Her arms and legs go wide like a psycho starfish, flying toward Austin and his family, halfway down the staircase.

Mateo doesn't even think before he leaps, intercepting Candy with a clumsy mid-air tackle.

Their tangled bodies plummet, and the next thing Mateo feels are the prickles of pine needles on his skin as he slams into the Christmas tree below, which collapses on him and Candy.

Austin screams, "Mateo!" from somewhere outside the mess of green branches.

Footsteps rush down the steps.

Mateo's empty hands scramble, trying to find the knife that was knocked loose in the fall.

Candy pops up from the wreckage like a jack-in-the-box, clutching something in her grip.

A shiny candy cane ornament with the long end broken into a porcelain point.

She rears it back, and Mateo steals one last glance out of the tree at Austin.

Not just the boy he has a crush on. The boy he loves.

It's the best last thing he could hope to see before the jagged ornament slams down into his eye socket, and everything cuts to black.

CHAPTER TWENTY

Dana holds her son back. Austin is screaming Mateo's name, trying to rush toward the tree to help the boy he loves, but Dana knows it's too late. The moment that ornament plunged into Mateo's head, his body went quiet and still.

She's had to process a lot of death tonight, and fast, but if she slows down now, it's all over.

"Austin, listen to me." She pulls Austin toward the basement door, opens it and guides him inside. "Your plan, it was a good one." She helps Fiona down the first step, passing her the crutches. "Find the truck keys and get out of here. I'll buy you some time."

"What?" Austin responds. "Mom, no we're not going anywhere without you."

"Fiona." Dana looks to her daughter, the strongest girl she's ever known. "Help your brother."

The look on both of their faces is too heartbreaking. If she waits another fraction of a second, she'll lose her will, so she slams the door on the only family she has left.

Austin's fist thumps against it. "Mom, don't! Come with us!"

Dana leans her head against the wood, listening to her daughter's steady voice on the other side: "Austin. I know you're sad. I'm sad too. But we have to move. Now."

Good girl, Fiona.

Dana puts her back against the basement door and slides down to the floor, creating a human barricade with her children on the other side.

If it's the last thing she does, she will protect them. But after what she's seen tonight, she knows a straight up fight with Candy Cain isn't going to end well. She has to find another way.

Dana tucks the kitchen knife out of sight under her leg just as Candy rises from the fallen Christmas tree, dripping with pine needles. The grown girl grips a new toy in her hand.

The silver star that once rested atop the tree.

Three sharp points protrude between Candy's fingers as she stalks across the room.

Dana looks over at Greg's body. Her North Star. She has to try to be what her husband wanted her to be. Even if she has to use her rusty acting skills to fake it. She's going to be warm and loving.

She's going to be Mother.

"Merry Christmas, Candace," Dana says. "You must have been so lonely all these years. So cold." She really needs to sell it, so she digs deep, searching for empathy. "I'm sure you didn't want to have to kill all those people tonight. But they came into your home, didn't they?"

Candy stops in her tracks. Cocks her head like she's actually thinking, feeling something other than a murderous rage.

It's working.

"You were just scared, right? Defending your home. Your mommy and daddy didn't treat you well. I saw it. In the video." Dana motions toward the couch, where Brock tossed the camcorder.

Candy's head swivels toward it. Is that a twinge of sadness, a frown behind the mask of black hair?

"Come here," Dana says, extending her arms. "Let me hold you."

Candy steps toward Dana, just a foot away now. She raises that silver star high.

Dana closes her eyes. At least she tried.

Smash.

She opens her eyes to find Candy empty-handed, the ornament shattered to silver fragments on the floor.

Dana's heart lodges in her throat as Candy slowly lowers into her lap. She cradles the lanky teenaged girl, rocking her back and forth. Candy smells awful up close, but Dana can't show disgust, can't show fear, even though she's utterly terrified.

She can only show love.

Dana raises her right hand to the girl's cheek, pushing the black hair away. The face beneath brings spicy vomit up her throat, but she chokes it down. Replaces it with kind words.

"You poor thing."

Candy clearly likes her Christmas carols, so Dana tries to remember one. The small town she grew up in didn't have a theater, so she got her acting start in Christmas pageants. Her memories from those early days are a blur, some of them more consciously scrubbed than others, but music has a way of sticking in the brain.

Dana keeps rocking the child in her arms and begins to sing.

"What child is this who laid to rest. . ."

Her left hand quietly lowers toward the floor.

". . . on Mary's lap is sleeping?"

She wraps her fingers around the knife handle. The metal blade makes a slight *tick* against the wooden floor as she lifts it. Candy doesn't seem to hear the sound, doesn't seem to notice Dana's hand moving up behind her head.

Candy hums along as Dana sings.

"Whom angels greet with anthems sweet. . ."

Dana hesitates, only for a moment. All that digging for warmth really has unearthed some empathy in her heart.

Can she really kill this child?

". . .while the good shepherds watch are keeping?"

She has no choice if she wants to protect her own children. She has to act, now.

But that one moment of hesitation is all it takes for Candy's body to tense in Dana's arms.

Just as Dana tries to thrust the knife down, Candy's fingers clamp around her hand. Sharp nails dig into flesh as Dana lets out a cry. She tries to release the knife, but Candy won't let her.

Candy looks up at the blade, frowning as she guides it toward the side of Dana's head and picks up the song.

"Oh raise, oh raise this song on high. . ."

The girl is strong, and Dana's arm feels weak, those ragged fingernails shredding the tendons in her hand as blood seeps.

"His mother sings her lullaby. . ."

The tip of the blade grazes Dana's ear lobe, landing softly in her inner ear. She tries to stop it, but Candy grabs the other side of Dana's head and pushes it further against the blade.

"Oh joy, oh joy, for Christ is born. . ."

The knife slices in, and Dana hears the flesh splitting just before her eardrum *pops*.

There's only ringing in that ear now, like a faint church bell, as the other ear catches Candy's final verse:

". . . the babe, the child of Mary."

The blade digs deeper and downward now, grazing Dana's jawbone as the cold metal glides through her jugular vein. Blood oozes over her ear, running down her neck.

Death comes quick, and Dana welcomes the warmth, pooling in her lap where the child still rests.

Candy watches the whites of Mother's eyes go red and gives her one last hug. It turns the white stripes on Candy's pajamas red now too.

She drags Mother across the floor, laying her next to Father.

The path to the basement door is clear now.

The door to her home, where the children wait.

CHAPTER TWENTY-ONE

Austin can barely hear Fiona's voice over the sound of his own sobbing, but he knows she's right.

They need to move. Now.

He puts everything that's happened tonight out of his mind, steels himself and turns toward his sister with a nod. The only thing that matters now is what they do next, so they take their first steps into the shadowy cellar.

"Rick's body has to be here somewhere." Austin searches the cavernous corners, but finds nothing. Just shelves and boxes.

"Austin." Fiona points a crutch at the little square door in the floor. The one Ethan almost opened earlier.

The one in the video where Mother was killed.

Austin wraps his fingers around the metal ring and gives it a big pull. The wood groans until the square door pops out of its frame, like opening the worst present ever.

The smell slams Austin in the face and he gags

instantly. Two corpses are folded up inside, a tangle of limbs improbably bent into the tight space.

"What is it?" Fiona asks far enough away that she can't see the crooked contents.

"Stay there." Austin doesn't want his sister to see any more bloodshed than she already has.

The body on top is definitely Lynette. He recognizes the beige pantsuit, even under the ropy red intestines that have been wrapped around her body like Christmas tree lights.

Austin gets onto his knees and starts tugging at her limbs. Rigor mortis has set in, so it takes a bit more effort than just pulling wrapping tissue from a gift box. He manages to move her body to the side, revealing the second one underneath. A man, facedown, the back half of his skull caved in. This must be Rick.

Austin starts digging, trying reach the front pockets of the man's overalls; but his searching fingers land on something he wasn't looking for beneath the body.

He pulls out an old children's Bible, stained with blood. The one Mother was clutching in the video. Austin tosses the book to the floor and keeps digging, elbow deep in dead bodies. His fingers finally slip into a denim pocket, touching cold metal.

"Holy shit." Austin pulls his hand out to show Fiona the dangling keys. "I actually found them."

"Great," Fiona says. "Because I'd like to get where we're going sometime before Christmas."

Austin's never appreciated his sister's sense of humor more. They share a sad little laugh before he rushes up to the metal storm doors. Pressing upward, he's met with some unexpected resistance.

"Damn, they're heavy. Must be the snow."

He resets his hands for a sturdier push. The gap between cracks opens a little further, releasing a red Slurpee mixture that drips down against Austin's grit teeth. He stumbles backwards, wiping his bloodied face.

"What is it?" Fiona asks.

Austin's just piecing it together himself, realizing why those doors won't open.

"It's Valerie. I think her body fell onto the doors. It's weighing them down with all the snow."

He gives it another try, shouldering one door and using his legs to lift, ignoring the slippery organs that slip through the crack to slap his face. But it's too much weight, and he collapses to the steps.

"I can't open them. We're stuck."

"We can't be stuck," Fiona says. "There has to be another way out." She looks around the space, nodding toward the raised rectangular window. "There."

Austin runs over. "That must be the window she crawled out of to get Ethan."

"If she can do it, so can we."

Austin uses the old wooden shelf like a stepping stool. Once he gets up to the window, he sees another six inches of fresh snow have already packed against the glass. He tries to open it, but it won't budge. "I think it's frozen shut."

"So, smash the fucking thing!" Fiona says.

Austin grabs a can of deviled ham off the shelf, gripping it as he wraps a dirty rag around his whole hand.

One punch doesn't do it.

Neither does two.

But on the third, his protected fist breaks through. Austin keeps smashing around the edge to remove the broken shards from the wooden frame. The image of Valerie's death is still emblazoned in his mind, and there will be no repeats of that. Once he's cleared every last sharp edge and pushed the snow away to make room on the other side, he climbs back down the rickety shelf.

"You first," he says to Fiona. He tries to give her a boost up the makeshift stepping stool, but she's struggling to pull herself up, even with his help.

"I can't," she says, tears of pain in her eyes. "You have to go first and pull me."

Austin climbs back up to the window. It's harder than it looks, pulling himself up through the small rectangle, but he manages to scramble out into the snow. He takes a deep breath of fresh air and turns back to his sister.

"Pass me the crutches first," he says. Fiona slides them up through the window one at a time. She manages to climb up high enough for Austin to latch onto her arms. "I've got you."

The old wooden shelf shakes beneath her wobbling legs. "Austin..."

He feels her grip slip as the shelf tips over. Fiona falls backward, sprawling out onto the ground amongst the spilled cans and boxes.

"Are you okay?" Austin asks.

She pushes up onto her forearms with that familiar refrain. "I'm fine."

The basement door *creeeaks* open above. Austin tenses at the sound.

"Mom?" he asks with undue hope.

No answer. Just slow footsteps.

That's enough to tell them both that their mother is gone.

"Austin." Fiona refocuses his attention, speaking up from the cold ground. "You have to go."

"No." Austin shakes his head. "No, I can't do that again, I won't."

The footsteps get closer to the bottom.

"Please." She's begging him now, tears streaming down her cheeks. "I don't want you to die because of me."

Those last three words cut Austin deep, echoing the cold thing he said to her before this nightmare began.

It'll be because of you.

Austin wishes he could go back and take those words back, but there's no time for that. All he can say now is what he should've said sooner.

"I'm sorry." He lowers the crutches back into the basement.

Fiona uses them to get back up on her feet. "I'm sorry too. Now, get out of here."

Candy Cain descends the final step, bare feet landing on the basement floor. She's clutching a hastily wrapped present that Austin can only assume is his mother's head, but he doesn't wait to find out.

He pushes away from the window, away from his vulnerable sister.

But he's not going to the truck. Not without her.

Austin hurries to the storm doors to discover his grim suspicions were right. Both halves of Valerie are piled across the doors, along with the heavy skillet and a whole lot of snow.

"I'm so sorry, Val." Austin drags his friend's torso off the doors, then does the same with her legs. He scrambles to clear the red snow before grabbing the skillet.

It still takes all his strength to pull one of the metal doors open, and he rushes down the steps.

Fiona's still standing, using those forearm crutches like swords. She throws alternating swings to keep her opponent at bay until Austin finally leaps between them.

"Get away from her!" He raises the skillet high.

Candy Cain cowers, giving Austin pause.

She holds out that lumpy present, wrapped with discarded paper. Austin stares at it for a moment, seeing it's too dry to be a head or any other severed body part.

Candy takes a step forward, pushing it toward him.

"I think she wants you to take it," Fiona says over his shoulder.

He considers slamming that skillet down on her skull, but he's seen how quick this girl is. She stopped attacking for a reason, so he needs to seize this strange peace offering.

Austin lowers his weapon to the ground, keeping his eyes on Candy as he takes the present from her gnarled hands.

Candy just stands there. Waiting.

Austin peels the wrapping paper away to reveal. . . the camcorder.

"Thank you," he says, confused.

Candy grunts, displeased.

"We already saw the video," Austin says. "We know what you did—"

The feral girl hisses. Austin steps back, shielding Fiona.

Candy's chapped lips press forward, parting that stringy black hair as she utters one word:

"Play."

Austin's hand trembles as he flips the LCD screen open and presses the 'Play' button.

It's cued up in the middle of the prank recording. Probably from when his parents watched it, or maybe when his dad showed it to Sheriff Brock.

Before Brock killed Dad.

Austin steals a glance up the steps toward the open door. His mother's body is collapsed there, blood flowing down the steps. Both of his parents are gone. One at the hands of that evil fucking cop, the other at the hands of this wild girl standing in front of him.

"Merry Christmas, motherfucker!"

Laughter buzzes from the speakers as Valerie, Ethan and Mateo reveal themselves on the video.

They're all dead too.

Fiona is all Austin has left, and he won't let Candy take her. He'll beat her to death with this camcorder if he has to.

But why is she making him—

The screen scrambles for a moment before cutting back into the original recording.

Young Candace sits there, petting her dead sister's hair as the fire blazes.

Austin understands now.

Valerie taped over a small segment of that fateful Christmas morning.

But the story wasn't over. . .

CHAPTER TWENTY-TWO

C andace hums *Away in a Manger* while the Christmas tree burns bright.

The flames lick off the branches and catch on Father first, smoke rising from his cooking corpse.

"Merry Christmas, Father," Candace says.

Mother catches next, orange flickers bouncing across her body to burn beside her husband.

"Merry Christmas, Mother."

Abby coughs on the ground. Still alive?

". . . Abby?" Candace leans over her sister, who's choking, gurgling blood that soaks her gorgeous blonde locks.

Candace just watches, shaking her head. "Go to sleep, Abby."

Whispered words bubble from Abby's lips, too soft to hear over the crackling flames.

"What was that?" Candace leans closer to her sister.

"Puh. . . present," Abby says.

Candace's eyes follow Abby's finger, pointing toward a box tucked far behind the flaming tree. It catches fire just before Candace snatches it up, swatting at the flames. She stamps out the embers with her bare hands and plucks the charred card.

"To Candace. The Best Sister Ever. Love Abby."

Candace peels the wrapping paper off. Slowly, lovingly. The only present she's gotten today. Maybe ever.

Her little hand reaches into the box and pulls out a custom snow globe. Inside the glass ball, two tiny figurines stand amidst the flurry of fake snow. A black-haired girl and a yellow-haired girl wearing red and white striped pajamas. Holding hands and smiling.

Candace starts to cry. Abby reaches up for the snow globe, and Candace lets her hold it.

"Thank you, Abby." She strokes her sister's cheek. "Merry Christmas."

"Merry. . ." Abby's arm stretches wide, clutching the globe. ". . . Christmas." She throws all of her energy into one big swing, smashing the glass ball against her sister's head. The force sends Candace flopping onto the flaming tree, where she screams and flails in the fiery branches.

Abby crawls toward the couch to pull herself up, grabbing the camera.

The lens points up at her busted face. Nose broken, eye swollen, teeth missing.

Over Abby's shoulder, a flaming Candace rises with a growl. She leaps toward Abby, who dodges her sister and darts toward the basement door, slamming it closed behind her. Abby holds the knob closed as the door shakes against Candace's fists, pummeling the door with fury.

Smoke rises beneath the crack of the door.

The slamming slows and ends with one heavy *thump*.

Abby takes a few steps down the stairs and aims the camera beneath the crack.

Candace's face melts into the wood like candle wax.

Abby runs down the wooden staircase and up the stone steps to the storm doors. She tries to push them open, but they're too heavy for the little girl to lift.

Sirens are screaming outside now, and Abby sees red lights flashing through the little basement window.

She scurries back down the steps, pacing in the basement.

"Naughty, Abby. Naughty."

She stops, zooms the camera in on the hatch in the floor.

Where naughty girls go.

Abby climbs into the space and pulls the square door into place, boxing herself in like a present. She clutches the bloodstained Bible, her security blanket.

Footsteps and banging upstairs. Men shout and fire-hoses blast.

Abby rocks back and forth in the dark. She stares into the camera and sings a Christmas carol to tune out the scary noises above.

"Away in a manger, no crib for a bed. . . The little Lord Jesus laid down His sweet head. . ."

CHAPTER TWENTY-THREE

Fiona looks up from the camcorder screen at the girl standing in front of her. She sees now that the dirty black hair has flecks of natural blonde color beneath all that soot and grime.

"You're not Candace."

The girl lowers her head, suddenly shy under Fiona's gaze.

"You're Abby."

"Why did you hide?" Austin asks. "When the firemen came? Why didn't you let them help you?"

Abby tilts her head back up, and the hair falls away to reveal her deformed face. It reminds Fiona of a Picasso painting, the nose and eye slightly shifted out of place. Candace may not have killed her sister with that coal, but there's no way Abby doesn't have some kind of brain damage beneath her cratered forehead.

Her chapped lips part to speak. "Abby. . . kill. . . Candace." A single tear slips out of her sunken eye. "Abby. . . naughty. . . girl."

Fiona's heart breaks for the tortured girl. Even

though it was Candace who killed their parents and tried to kill her sister, it's Abby who considers herself the villain, just for defending herself.

Because she was supposed to be the good girl.

Nobody would've blamed her, especially with the video evidence; but all that trauma, all that guilt kept Abby locked away in this house for ten years.

Fiona looks around at the basement, packed with canned goods and water. Abby's doomsday Christian parents had unwittingly created the perfect home for her. Until Lynette came in, took Abby's home, and unboxed a monster.

Abby sees the Bible on the ground and stoops to pick it up. She runs her hand along the bloodstained cover and looks up at the window, where a pink dawn breaks through the trees.

Abby hands Austin the Bible. "Merry. . . Christmas."

He takes it, looking to Fiona with a *What's happening?* glance while responding: "Merry Christmas. . ."

Before Fiona can finish shrugging, Abby is scooping her up into those surprisingly strong arms. Fiona's crutches fall to the ground as Abby carries her toward the stairs.

"Hey!" Austin bends down to reach for the skillet.

Fiona shakes her head, mouthing "Don't." She doesn't know what's happening, but she knows Abby hasn't killed them yet, so they just have to play along for now.

Austin seems to understand as he leaves the skillet, carrying the camcorder and Bible as he follows Abby and Fiona upstairs.

As they pass into the living room, Fiona catches sight of the knife handle protruding from her mother's ear. At least she's been lain next to her father. Fiona tries to focus her attention on Abby, who's setting her down now beside the fallen tree.

Abby guides Austin to the couch and sits him there with the camcorder. She opens the Bible to a specific page and places it in his lap. Then she hits 'Rewind' on the camcorder to roll the tape all the way back before pressing the 'Record' button.

Abby nods to Austin, as if to say, "You know what to do."

But he doesn't seem to understand until Fiona speaks up. "I think she wants to recreate that Christmas morning. To rewrite her history."

Fiona understands that impulse. Wishing that you could just erase all the pain and start fresh. A new life.

She can't bring her parents back, but maybe if they have a Merry Christmas with Abby, nobody else has to die.

Fiona gives her brother an encouraging nod. He settles into his role and starts filming.

Abby reaches into the pocket of her pajama pants and pulls out a lump of coal. Probably that same lump of coal from ten years ago. A gruesome keepsake.

She places the rock in Fiona's hand.

"Thank you," Fiona says, unsure of what else to say. "This is a very nice Christmas present."

Abby shakes her head. She takes Fiona's hand and guides it toward her own dented skull. Abby motions up and down in a violent gesture.

"You want me to hit you?" Fiona asks.

Abby nods, singing softly. *"And take us to Heaven. . ."*

"She's not rewriting the story," Austin says from behind the camera. "She's wrapping it up. She wants you to finish what her sister started." He's looking down at the open Bible in his lap, reading aloud now. "Cain said to the Lord, 'My punishment is more than I can bear. Today you are driving me from the land, and I will be hidden from your presence; I will be a restless wanderer on the earth, and whoever finds me. . . will kill me.'"

Fiona shakes her head at the brutal Bible verse. "No. I won't do it."

Abby sings louder, more commanding. *"And take us to Heaven!"*

"Fiona," Austin calls from the couch. The camcorder shakes in his hands. "You have to finish it."

Abby takes Fiona's hand and uses it to *thump* the coal against her own head.

"Take!"

Thump.

"Us!"

Thump.

"To!"

Fiona releases her grip, and the coal rolls to the floor as she yanks her hand back.

"You don't have to do this, Abby," Fiona says. "We can get you help."

Abby shrieks and grabs the coal. She rears her arm back, aiming for Fiona's head.

Out of the corner of her eye, Fiona sees her brother

dropping the camera and leaping from the couch to stop what comes next. But she knows he won't make it in time, won't save her.

That's not how this story ends.

CHAPTER TWENTY-FOUR

"Fiona!" Austin screams, arms outstretched as he scrambles from the couch, trying desperately to get between her and that black rock of death.

He stumbles, falls. When he looks up from the floor, Fiona's face is red with blood.

Austin's whole body shakes with agony, until he realizes...

That's not her blood.

The tip of the fireplace poker is jutting out from Abby's chest. She looks down at it, drops the coal.

Austin follows the iron rod behind Abby to see Mateo gripping the handle from where he lies among the pine needles. The candy cane ornament is still stuck in his eye as he asks: "Did I get her?"

Abby collapses sideways onto the tree, and Austin rushes to pull Mateo up to his feet.

"Holy shit, you're alive."

"Yeah, I guess I kinda blacked out." Mateo rubs the side of his head. "What'd I miss?"

Fiona wipes Abby's blood from her face. "The worst nativity play ever. Will someone grab me my cane?"

Austin finds it beside the couch and helps his sister to her feet. He drapes Mateo's arm around his neck and the three of them head for the front door. Austin cuts the bungee cord, freeing them to head down the porch steps and out into the dawn.

"I'll pull the car around," he says, holding up Rick's keys.

"Wait," Fiona says.

Austin follows his sister's gaze to the headless sheriff beneath the burnt husk of a station wagon. Brock's charred arm is extended in the snow, inches from the Zippo lighter.

Austin bends down and picks up the lighter, reading his sister's mind. "Are you sure? Mom and Dad are in there."

"Mom and Dad are gone," Fiona says. Austin's too numb to cry right now, but he knows the grief will come later. "And you were right. We have to finish this."

He takes a deep breath, then flicks the flame and tosses the Zippo onto the porch where Brock poured all that gasoline. It lights quickly, the entire front of the house turning into a wall of flames.

The warmth feels good as he puts a hand on Mateo's cheek, inspecting the ornament in his eye. "Does it hurt?"

"Only when I blink."

Neither of them can help laughing.

"You still have a crush on me?" Mateo asks.

"Captain Morgan is basically our cupid, so I guess I have a thing for pirates."

"Argh?" Mateo squints.

"Argh." Austin grins.

Fiona rolls her eyes. "Will you two kiss already?"

Austin leans forward, carefully navigating around the protruding porcelain to find Mateo's lips.

This time, Mateo kisses back, and Austin's heart blooms.

A human screech echoes from inside the house, and all three of them turn toward the flaming porch.

Abby bursts from the open door, through the fire. Her pajamas are melting into her skin, her body in full-on flames as she charges across the snow with the fire poker still skewered through her. Arms outstretched toward Austin and Mateo, running fast, aiming to add them to her human kebab when—

Crack.

Fiona's cane connects with Abby's neck in a bone-crunching swing that knocks the cooked killer off her feet.

"Go to Heaven," Fiona says to Abby's still body, smoldering in the snow with wide eyes staring endlessly into the heavens above.

Fiona stumbles, but Austin jumps to her side to hold her up.

"Sorry, I know," Austin says. "You're fine."

"No," his sister responds. "I'm not."

Fiona releases her cane to wrap her arms around her brother, and they cry. Deep, guttural. After everything they've lost, it feels good to release some sorrow, to embrace what they still have left.

Mateo waits patiently until the catharsis is over. He scoops up the cane and hands it back to Fiona. "Nice swing."

Crack.

This time it's the roof of the house collapsing in on itself. The stone exterior stands like an open fire pit now, nothing but burning debris within. A campfire where children might tell the tale of Candy Cain.

But she'll be nothing more than a legend now.

Austin stares at her corpse in the snow. "Why don't we all go get the truck together?"

"Yeah, I think that's a good idea," Mateo agrees.

The sun is rising over the treetops as they head around back to the truck. Mateo helps Fiona climb into the middle, then gets in beside her, exhaling deeply. "I could really use some hot chocolate right now."

Austin starts the engine. "We know an awful all-night diner."

"Sounds perfect."

They drive away from the burning house in silence.

A screaming firetruck passes them on the snowy road into town, but Austin pays it no mind. He just pulls right up to the diner, single-minded in his purpose.

As they climb out of the truck, the church bell rings across the street. Austin turns to see Pastor Wendell, barely recognizable now, clean-shaven and sober. He greets the community as they stream in for Christmas morning service.

Wendell waves toward the kids. "Merry Christmas!"

"Merry Christmas!" Austin shouts. "Candy Cain is dead!"

The pastor's face goes whiter than the freshly fallen snow. He scurries into the church, away from Austin's gaze.

Sheriff Brock confessed a coverup, but it had to be bigger than just one man. There's no way Pastor Wendell didn't know about the abuse happening in the Thornton house. No way he and his congregation weren't turning a blind eye to the true horror before it boiled to a head.

Austin has half a mind to storm into the church right now, give that good Christian community a piece of his mind. Shout down their sins from the pulpit.

They created Candy Cain. They're all responsible, guilty.

Naughty, Austin thinks, a red and white bloodlust flashing behind his eyes.

He shakes it off, following his hunger into the diner behind Fiona and Mateo.

Grace greets them with a smile. "Merry Chris-my-God, your eye!" She gasps at Mateo. "Is it okay?"

"I really don't think so," Mateo responds.

Austin slides into the booth across from Fiona. "Three hot chocolates please, Grace."

The three of them sit in silence as *Jingle Bells* blares over the diner speakers.

Bells on bobtails ring
Making spirits bright
What fun it is to ride and sing
A sleighing song tonight, oh!

Grace returns with three mugs, eyeing the blood on

everybody's clothing. "Do you need me to call the sheriff?"

Austin wraps his hands around the steaming mug. "Sheriff's off duty."

Fiona points up toward the speakers. "All we need is for you to turn off this music."

"I get it," Grace nods. "I'm tired of Christmas songs too." She heads behind the counter, switching off the radio.

Austin raises his mug to Fiona and Mateo. They all *clink* and take the first sip of hot chocolate together. Sitting with the silence, enjoying their sugary treat.

"So," Fiona finally speaks up. "What do we do now?"

As if in response to her question, the church organ kicks in across the street. A choir's muted song drifts into the diner.

"Away in a manger, no crib for a bed. . . The little Lord Jesus laid down His sweet head. . ."

Austin's rage swells once again toward all of Nodland. He sees it in Fiona's eyes too, and Mateo's eye.

He kills the dregs of his hot chocolate, licking the gritty residue from his lips. "Why don't we have one more cup of cocoa. . . then go to church and raise some hell?"

Fiona smiles across the table at her brother.

"Amen."

CHAPTER TWENTY-FIVE

By the time the firefighters arrive on the scene, the Thornton house is hardly a house anymore.

They make quick work with the hose, putting out the smoldering pile of stones, and waste no time sifting through the wreckage.

Priority one is counting the bodies.

There's two in the living room, melted together in an almost-romantic scene.

Another one (or, really, two halves of one) out back by the storm door.

A little further out toward the back woods is the boy half-buried in snow. A terrible way to go.

Then there's the headless sheriff beneath the burned-up vehicle out front.

Not far from him is the strangest sight of all, carved into the snow. Something like a blackened snow angel where a burning body once was.

The firefighters are wondering what the hell happened here, unaware of the guardian angel silently watching them from the edge of the woods. If any of those helmeted heads did turn that way, all they'd see from this distance is a shadowy figure leaning on a cane.

But it's not a cane, exactly. It's a blood-stained fire poker, gripped by a charred black hand. The flesh around it has fused with the tattered cotton remnants of red and white striped pajamas.

Her parents called her Abby, but she doesn't want their name anymore.

She has a new name now. One she heard shouted through the house, all night long.

One she now hears whispered off the lips of those firemen.

Candy Cain smiles at the big red firetruck that Santa brought her, full of so many toys.

She opens her scorched mouth to sing, *"Christmas time is here."*

STOP ■

ACKNOWLEDGMENTS

Candy Cain would have never come knocking at my
brain door if it wasn't for Alan Lastufka. When he
pitched me the Killer VHS Series concept and asked if I'd
be interested in writing one, I could hardly resist such an
inspiring creative prompt. It's been a dream to collabo-
rate with a passionate and innovative publisher who
treats books not as content or IP, but as works of art.

Speaking of art: How about that cover, right?! Marc
Vuletich has my deep gratitude for handcrafting a VHS
throwback vibe beyond my wildest nightmares, as do
Nancy Lefever and Erin Foster for helping hone my
words to a sharpened boxcutter edge. Thanks to my
agent, Dan Milaschewsi, for encouraging me to follow
the fire that's burning brightest.

I'm eternally grateful to my parents for never
censoring which tapes I plucked from the Horror shelves
at The Movie Store, and to my brother and sister for
always playing nice.

Morgan, I love you. You are my chosen family, my
forever home.

The greatest gift of all is writing books for *you*, dear

reader. Thank you for joining me on this wicked slay ride.
I hope it makes your spirits bright, even in the darkest
night.

Merrily Yours,
Brian McAuley

ABOUT THE AUTHOR

Brian McAuley is a WGA screenwriter whose produced credits range from family sitcoms to horror films. His debut novel *Curse of the Reaper* was named one of the Best Horror Books of 2022 by Esquire. Brian's short fiction and non-fiction have appeared in Dark Matter Magazine, Nightmare Magazine, and Shortwave Magazine. He received his MFA in Film from Columbia University and teaches at Arizona State University. Connect with him on social media @BrianMcWriter

A NOTE FROM SHORTWAVE

Thank you for reading the second Killer VHS Series book! If you enjoyed *Candy Cain Kills*, please consider writing a review. Reviews help readers find more titles they may enjoy, and that helps us continue to publish titles like this.

For more Shortwave titles, visit us online...

OUR WEBSITE

shortwavepublishing.com

SOCIAL MEDIA

@ShortwaveBooks

EMAIL US

contact@shortwavepublishing.com

REWIND AND EXPERIENCE THE
KILLER VHS SERIES
FROM THE BEGINNING...

ALEX EBENSTEIN

AVAILABLE NOW
EVERYWHERE BOOKS ARE SOLD!

ALSO AVAILABLE FROM SHORTWAVE PUBLISHING

ALSO AVAILABLE FROM SHORTWAVE PUBLISHING

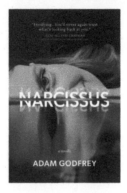
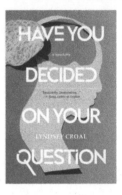

ALSO AVAILABLE FROM SHORTWAVE PUBLISHING

ALSO AVAILABLE
FROM
SHORTWAVE PUBLISHING

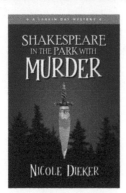

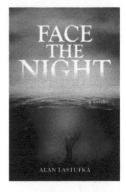

Milton Keynes UK
Ingram Content Group UK Ltd.
UKHW040301301024
450244UK00002B/8